# THE TWINS

NJ MOSS

BLOODHOUND
— BOOKS —

# 1

## LORNA

*I know what your husband does to you when the lights go out. Or in the sun if he thinks nobody's watching.*

On the back: an address, this café. The note's stabbing my eyes. Not literally, but that's how it feels each time I look at it. My dad would've called that absurdly dramatic. He hated metaphor and anything that wasn't blunt, a tool, practical.

We've been so careful, me and Malcolm, about the hidden sickness in our marriage. It's impossible for anybody else to know, but still, there it is, clutched in my hand as I look around the café.

I'm sitting on the seafront of Weston-super-Mare, a newish town for us, as far from the mess back home as we could get. It's on the southwest of England, facing the setting sun: the light in which this apparent observer witnessed Malcolm…

What did they see, I wonder?

Maybe it was the time he *disciplined* me behind the off-licence, because I begged him not to drink, reminded him he was driving home. Or it could've been the time we were stood between the alleyway of two clubs, and I said something silly, masochistic really, about his manhood. That was in the dark, though.

The café is quiet. The decorations are red, the seats red, everything reminding me of blood.

I can't think who could've left this note. It was waiting on the doormat, five or so minutes after Malcolm left for work. They must've watched him leave, then sneaked over, slid it through the letter box.

Another sip of coffee; another jolt of anxiety right to the heart.

Facing the window, the sun glints, blinds, then the glass door opens. It's happening again. Reality is tearing at the edges. I think of Scotland, of new starts, of my parents, of the strange path my life has taken. The bruise beneath my blouse throbs as I stare at her.

It's impossible. *She's* impossible. My double walks across the café, pauses at my table. "Hi, sis," the stranger says, grinning.

She's five and a half foot. Her eyes are pale green; Malcolm used to romantically say mine were forests and he wanted to disappear into them. But that was in the beginning. Her lips are slightly asymmetrical, giving her a lopsided smile. Her hair is different, dyed pink, a punky bob, and I'd never wear those loud-coloured green jeans, or the strappy leather top, but it's her: a mirror.

I'm staring at myself. The other woman sits. I'm honestly wondering if anybody else can see her. "It's nice to meet you. Now, let's talk about how I can save your life."

# 2

## SADIE

This is eerie. This woman is so much like me. That's a stupid thing to say, really, because I knew she would be.

I wasn't sure I wanted to meet her. And anyway, I was in no state. I'm still withdrawing now, but the worst of the shakes have stopped. It's hard to focus. I've got to do this.

Lorna wasn't raised by a powerful, kind woman. She didn't spend her childhood sharing ice cream and watching films and dancing together and becoming friends as much as mother and daughter. She didn't cry when Mum, *my* mum, the woman who adopted me – Olivia – died, until her eyes felt like they were bleeding.

I've seen Lorna before, of course, but this is so much more shocking, the closeness, and the fact she can see me. It's somehow stranger than hiding in the shadows.

"My name's Sadie," I say, when Lorna just sits there. "And before you ask, yes, I'm the one who left the note."

"Obviously it was you."

"No need to be rude."

I smile. I'm not enjoying this, exactly, but there's a thrill to it. Sort of like the first time I snorted a line of coke. But I'm not so naïve anymore; I know the initial rush will fade. And anyway, I've got no choice. I can't waste time building some hollow sister-like relationship.

"Would you like another coffee?" I ask.

She shakes her head in a bizarre slow fashion, almost as if she's expecting me to turn to mulch and slide through my chair. I go to the counter, waiting behind an elderly man and his smiling Jack Russell terrier. I grin at the dog, waving my fingers.

I know Lorna's gripped with terror. I can't afford to care. But it does gnaw at me, a little. But there's no choice. I worked as a journalist (of sorts) for a while in my early twenties, and then I took a story about heroin… and then, lo and behold, *I* got hooked on the stuff.

It was a dark time. It led to some depressing places. So, I've got to keep going, stay clean. I've got fourteen days so far. That's the longest in a while. I proved something to myself. When I *need* to, I can get my act together.

After ordering a latte, I return to the table. Lorna doesn't look pleased. She smooths her mousy-brown hair from her face. It makes me wonder if my roots are coming through, and there it'll be, that same colour.

"Did you know, we're not just identical in appearance. We share the exact same DNA."

"Who cares?" Lorna says.

Her accent sounds almost completely Scottish when she gets passionate. That could be a problem. I sound like a well-educated, but not *too* posh English person.

"If you think about it, it's like we share the same soul."

# 3

## LORNA

And now the double is talking about souls, in an accent so different from mine.

I can't keep wondering if I'm going mad. She's sitting right in front of me. I could reach out and touch her, and then I *do*. Just the back of her hand, a graze of my fingertips. She doesn't seem surprised.

"I know," she says. "It's difficult to process. It's like staring at a robot. A copy."

"Are you a smoker?"

She winces. "Sometimes."

That feels like a victory, however small. "I've never touched cigarettes. I can hear it in your voice. You should quit."

"They're good for relieving stress."

"Just tell me what you want."

"This isn't about me. It's about you. It's about Malcolm using you as a punching bag whenever he feels like it. It's about last week, when you went to a pub, and the pub turned to a club... and what he did to you in the alleyway after."

The bruise pulses again, a memory of how I got it. A flash:

Malcolm's gritted teeth, his red face. And me just wanting it to end.

I was strong once, in the beginning. I'm sure I was. I hate the way I think about myself, anticipating the next *discipline*. That's what he does in public; imagine what he does at home.

"You want to escape your marriage."

The café is almost empty, just an old man and his dog. The dog barks loudly, the noise annoying, stabbing at my aching head, just like the note stabs at my eyes, and suddenly I'm shaking it, waving the note in her face. But even so, I keep my voice low.

Malcolm can't find out about this.

"If you know what's happening to me, you're sick for leaving this."

Sadie stares at the note. "I left you that note so you'd know I was serious. I can help you."

I don't want to listen to any of this. It's too surreal. I spend most of my time hiding these days, alone in the house watching television box sets. Cleaning, maybe doing a little painting and cooking. I try to workout, do yoga, meditate, a simple, boring, lonely life. It would be one of complete comfort, if it weren't for Malcolm coming home.

"You're scared to leave. Malcolm will find you."

*You must be psychic*, I almost say, but sarcasm is pointless.

She claws at a coaster, a golden crown on a red background, chipping away pieces of it. Her other hand is fidgeting with her coffee. "When I saw him hit you, I knew it wasn't the first time. It was your reaction. You hardly even flinched. You took it, leaned over a little…"

She knows she's hurting me. I can see it in her eyes, *my* eyes. "I've met men like him before. I'd wager he's been doing it for years, perhaps as long as you've been together. When I found y–"

"How *did* you find me?"

She doesn't respond immediately, seeming like she's deciding whether or not to tell the truth. Then she gently shrugs. "My mum passed away a few years ago. On her deathbed, she told me I was a twin. I paid a friend to track you down. He found your hometown, and spoke to somebody there, who mentioned Glasgow, and then from Glasgow to here."

"A friend," I repeat.

That's not good. How much digging did this *friend* do when they were following the trail of my life?

"What else did he tell you?"

"Just that you live here."

"Why do you know people who can do that sort of thing?"

The idea of people snooping around in my past makes me sick. But there's nothing I can do about it now. She doesn't *seem* to know anything more than that, but she could be hiding it well.

If she knew the truth, the reasons for running, she'd be disgusted, surely.

Sometimes it's hard to imagine what a regular person would feel. Not me, a hermit, a punching bag.

She's right. I wish I could escape.

"I've met all kinds of people in my life. Some of them, I wish I hadn't. Others have been useful. That's what I'm going to be for you, Lorna: useful."

"By following me. Stalking me."

"I had to see what you were, *who* you were, before I reached out. I'm sorry."

"I'm sure you are."

So much for my sarcasm rule.

"I take it you know you were adopted?" Sadie says. "You don't seem very surprised."

I say nothing; I won't tell her about the countless times my dad threw it in my face. The arguments. The crap. They treated me like I was a pet, not a person.

"Malcolm would find you if you left. He'd take you back. Or break you if you refused to go, so nobody else could have you."

There's nothing to say. It's all true.

"But what if he never knew you'd gone?" she says. "What if somebody could take your place?"

# 4

## SADIE

I've learned how to make what I say impactful. It's one of the skills of being a junkie, a surprising positive. Getting what I want, need, with the right combination of words. Sometimes, that can be flirtatious, suggestive. Or violent. Or anything in between.

It depends on the person; reading them is all part of the game.

Is it ironic that I've misread Lorna?

I expected her to be far meeker, based on how she'd behaved when I was watching her. But that was when she was the terrified housewife, slotted perfectly into her role.

She's got a flicker of... of *me* now, when she clenches her jaw.

"Why would you take my place? You've seen what my life is like."

"I want to help you." I soften, using a murmuring sweet voice, a voice that promises that its owner would never hurt anybody. "My mum didn't just tell me about you when she..."

I pretend to push away a sob. It's not all make-believe.

Whenever I think of Mum, looking so tiny in her bed, the sheets clinging to her skeletal form, real sadness touches me. But I keep it down deep, along with the voices screaming at me; one to use drugs and the other telling me that I shouldn't be doing this.

There's no coming back from this.

I should stop, and I push on. "She made me promise to help you. It was one of her biggest regrets, separating twins. She was a twin herself, and she valued that relationship more than anything."

Lorna narrows her eyes. But she doesn't say anything. I wonder if she's bought it, or if I should've thought of another reason. Suddenly I'm questioning my whole demeanour. I could've approached her kindly, won her trust, but I've let my habits take over.

I can save this. "The truth is, I don't want to be doing this. But I loved my mum more than life itself. I promised her, and it's a promise I will never, ever break. And I've done some... bad things in my life. I want to do some good."

Lorna isn't giving much away. She stares at me for a long time, then finally says, "You don't know what you're asking. It's not just the things you've seen."

"Don't worry. I can handle myself."

Lorna laughs, but there's no humour in it. "You really don't understand."

In a different world, I'd have time to learn. We could delve into each other's personalities, histories, mining little pieces of each other to inflate the lie. But I don't have that luxury.

"I've just moved here. I've got a flat. Some cash to tide me over. You could do anything. Start afresh without ever wondering if Malcolm would follow you. Think about it, Lorna. How insane is this? Me, you, sitting here. How absolutely mental?"

When Lorna smiles, it seems genuine, and I feel like I've won something. There's an uncanny connection I have to stubbornly deny. "Yeah, it is."

"He would never, in a million years, think to himself, *My wife has been replaced by her twin.* It's too absurd. So he'll never question it."

"Your accent is different," Lorna says. "Your hair isn't the same colour or length or style. And you don't know anything about us."

I'm getting tired of this now. My temper's ready to snap, but I try to ignore it. It's not just Lorna. It's the wind and the blaring coffee machine and the pounding between my ears. But it's mostly her.

"Those are my problems. We have to do this soon. Now. Tomorrow."

Lorna sits up. *"Tomorrow?"*

I nod. "I've been trying to put it off, to tell myself your life isn't that bad. But I can't, especially not after all I've seen. I have to help you."

"You'd really do that? Be with *him,* just because you promised your mum?"

"If you have to ask that, you must not have been blessed with a mother as perfect as mine."

I'm laying it on thick, but I've played this all wrong. From the start. A kind introduction letter would've been the best thing. But then, what if she told somebody that her *twin* had reached out? I couldn't risk that.

She has to believe me. This lie, which is, frankly, ridiculous. "Do you believe in God?" Lorna asks.

"I've never given it much thought."

And I don't want to now. Need to keep this moving. Less chance I'll care, less time for certain things to catch up to certain people. But that's why I've nearly messed this up, my distance, my blunt nature. Life's far less jagged when you spend half of it dulled with potions.

That's what a friend of mine used to call our fix. Potions.

He's dead now – overdose.

Lorna has an annoying habit of pausing before she speaks, as if for dramatic effect, like anybody cares. I'm tapping my fingernails against my saucer like mad, to the point where I hear the *click-click-click* and almost want to snap at the person to stop it.

"I always have," she says. "We went to church every day when I was a girl." Her eyes take on a far-away look. I wonder – hope – I look that magnetic when I'm lost in thought. "I believe God led you here, to me. It all aligns too perfectly. At the time I need you most, you come for me. If you're really willing to put yourself in *his* way, Sadie, then thank you. And thank God for sending you to me."

Oh, this is good. Lucky. I don't care what she has to believe to accept this. A pink dildo could've given her this prophecy, as long as she does what I need.

Even if it means the end of her life. Can I live with that? It's better than dying.

# 5

## LORNA

S adie is full of shit. I don't believe this for a second. Something's going on, maybe those *bad things* she mentioned.

If I become her, those bad things will be mine.

Goodbye four-bedroom house, with all the amenities a woman could wish for. Goodbye conservatory where I can do my yoga. Goodbye foot bath and the waterfall shower and all the luxuries that just about make this life worthwhile, sometimes, on a good week.

Or that's what I tell myself. I'd be out in the wild, alone, having to fend for myself. I'd have to switch on fierce parts of me. And hope reality doesn't bleed. Or if it does, it weeps for me, to my advantage.

Goodbye *Malcolm*, most of all. Whatever happens in this new Sadie chapter, it can't be worse than living with him another day. It's not just the hitting. It's the fact of him, my history reflected in his eyes, everything we've ever done, said, right there inside the other person.

I've tried to leave. Three times. But he won't let go. I'm scared of him. That's the shameful truth. I can't make him stop. I can't bring myself to do it.

Sadie can be his punching bag instead. She hasn't thought her plan through very well. For whatever reason – and I can think of a couple – she's pushing for this to be done quickly. What happens when Malcolm speaks to her, and she doesn't answer in the exact way he likes?

I'm going to play Sadie's game. She can keep her little lie. Whatever happens, this is my escape. I can face anything else. I can become who I need to be.

"How do we do this?" I ask.

Sadie's eyes gleam. She clearly thinks she's tricked me. She's revelling in it. "It's simple. I dye my hair back to its original colour. You cut yours, dye it, and go to my flat. We simply walk into each other's lives. I haven't got a job at the moment, but I've got money for a few months. You'll be able to find something. It's an adventure, Lorna."

She's talking persuasively, salesperson chatter. She doesn't know I've seen right through her.

"It's not me I'm worried about. I'm fairly confident I could survive your life."

A flicker at the corner of her eye, holding back her reaction. I hope I'm not this easy to read. "There's nothing to survive. Just a regular, boring life."

"Is your CV up to date?"

She flinches. I'm betting she's a drug addict. Or maybe she was one. It's the jittery movements, and she always seems on the verge of erupting. "I can type one up. But this has to be soon."

She couldn't be any more obvious if she tried. She's running from something: from her past. But so am I. Whatever else, it's change, finally. I won't have to ever kiss him, hold him, pretend to love him again.

Sadie's lying her way into hell. It's madness. She thinks whatever she's fighting is worse than *him*. Or me.

"Let's do it. I'll dye my hair." I take a long breath, as if steadying myself, and I am, but I'm also playing it up a bit. If she sees me as a mouse, let her. "I'm ready to start fresh. I'm ready to begin a new chapter."

I don't care if this is a dream. If my mind is playing its not-so-funny games. Just the thought of it, flying away from my life, disappearing into somebody else's, brings a smile to my face.

"I'm so grateful to your mum. She'd be so proud of you, Sadie. You're saving me."

But Sadie must truly not be very intelligent. Or perhaps she really is cracked out of her eyeballs. She didn't even explain *how* her mother, on her deathbed, supposedly knew I needed help. She could've spun some lie, mentioned a private detective, but she just fed me shit and expected me to eat it.

"We shouldn't meet in public again. Here." She reaches into her loud-coloured jeans, takes out a slip of paper. "There's a hotel roughly in between us. I've booked a room. I figure we could go there, say our last goodbyes, and then…"

"And then I can start my new life."

"He'll never hurt you again." She places her hand on mine, and even if I know this is a trick – an insultingly obvious one, honestly – I welcome the contact. "I didn't get to be your sister, but I can now. I can protect you."

"Thank you so, so much."

Is there anything real in this moment, or are we both faking, pretending to be people we're not?

"I have an idea," I say. "Let's both write some notes for each other. We'll do it tonight, a book of facts. At least then, we'll have a head start."

She should be more suspicious about how willing I am, how apparently gullible. I think she's used to viewing herself as better than others. She's underestimating me.

"That's a great idea." She stands, nods tightly, smiles in a half-true way. "See you tomorrow."

I walk around the table and hug her. There's too much stiffness in it for a moment, but then she remembers her role, and I remember mine too; I pull her close and thank her again.

When the hug ends, I miss it, just for a second. Maybe that's why I warn her. It's only fair. Whatever reason she has for this performance, it can't be more terrifying than her new life with Malcolm. And I could make it worse, if I wanted. Do I want that?

"Malcolm is not a good man. I'm giving you a chance, Sadie. You ca–"

"Can *do* this," she says firmly. "I'm not backing down. I'm ready. I want to do some good in my life."

"Then I'll see you tomorrow."

I leave the café, walk down the sunny promenade, and suddenly the bruise under my ribs doesn't hurt so much.

# CROSSED LINES

You'll say I made you this way.

When you've crossed lines you never dreamed you could, when you've done things religious people would call sinful, you'll blame me. But the truth is, I'm a sculptor, and all I did was hammer a block of stone until it bled.

I'm not trying to be melodramatic. I'm a seriously sadistic person. I've got tendencies that we could discuss, perhaps mentioning nature versus nurture and whether the world sharpens the sword or if it's the other way around.

But I stopped apologising for being me a long time ago. I am who I am and I don't give a damn, thank you, ma'am, and let's talk about all the sick shit *you've* done.

I'm not being playful. I've never honestly been very playful.

Here's a solid principle: there are some people blessed with the ability to enjoy inflicting pain. It's a curious, addictive pleasure, and only a few are born with the right genes, or predisposition, or whatever you want to call it, to feel it.

I can feel it. And so can you. You can't change. You can never change.

All the bad things you've ever done define you. They *are* you.

You're filth. You're not art. You're nothing. I'm not deranged. You are. The world is.

The world's weeping and the tears are dissolving reality, and I can detach, become nothing, and I can feel Every. Single. Fucking. Moment. I'm shouting now, roaring like a god, like a Viking berserker, beating my chest. Nobody knows who I really am.

Only the rare few who look me in the eye before I kill them. But not you. Never you. Because you're like me. And I love you for it, in my own way.

# 6

## SADIE

That went better than expected. I've already arranged my haircut, and I go straight there after meeting with Lorna. I've rented a flat in Bristol, a city near Weston, so I was close enough but not too far to make following her difficult.

It *was* difficult, though, especially with the drugs calling to me, the goddamn adrenaline. People don't get that. It pumps a person up, a survival mechanism, telling them if they don't get what they need, they'll die. *I'll* die.

But now I'm going to live. I did it: drove to Weston, watched her large house on the hill, near the woods, looking down on the peasants and the sea. She spends her days doing whatever she likes, and her only problem is an average-looking man.

Malcolm is in his fifties, if I had to guess, definitely older than Lorna and me – we're thirty-five – but not quite *cradle robber* territory. He works as a senior financial consultant.

Malcolm is nothing compared to the men I've dealt with. Lorna might have her timid warnings, but I refuse to believe this man with the receding hairline, the bulge in his belly, his demeanour defeated and depressed, is anything compared to the horror chasing me.

The horror which might end up getting Lorna killed.

Walking into the hairdressers, I smile as a teenager approaches, a blonde with big, innocent, kind eyes. Nothing bad has ever happened to her, and suddenly I feel so guilty for what I'm going to do.

Lorna is soft. She's become so accustomed to the walls of her existence, she mistakes them for the entire world. She shouldn't have agreed so quickly; I expected more pushback. But she believes her situation is *that* dire. She seeks solace in religion because her life is so unbearable. She thinks Malcolm is scarier than what's coming for her.

But that's not fair. I lied. I'll have to lie some more, in this book of facts we're going to gift each other. I can't tell the truth.

The hairdresser leads me over to the chair, asking if I've watched a recent episode of a show I've never heard of. I'm about to try and make some polite small talk when a familiar sickness grips me.

"Where's the bathroom, please?" I say, cutting off her story.

She points urgently, sympathy in her innocent face. She could be thinking of her first period, an embarrassment in school, and perhaps that's the worst thing that's ever happened to *her*. That's how some people work: the worst thing is, to their mind, the most evil thing imaginable.

This hairdresser is one of these people, and Lorna is another.

I puke all over the toilet bowl, flush it, then close the seat and sit. My hand comes to rest on my belly, and I let myself feel a tiny flicker of excitement, of hope. I'm not just doing this for me.

As deranged as it is, my baby will have a better life with Malcolm.

# 7

---

## LORNA

I'm still wondering if this is reality bleeding at the edges again. It's never been this bad before, never this vivid.

As I walk from my car to a large detached four-bedroom home – the garden perfect, the brickwork gleaming, everything flawless, everything proclaiming to our neighbours that we're respectable, *good* people – I imagine showing up at the hotel tomorrow, finding nothing but my own reflection.

But realistically, what are the chances I sat in a café, talking to myself?

Opening the front door, I mutter a silent promise I'll make tonight as loving as it can be. Malcolm and I will forget all the bad things we've ever done. We'll simply be together. Hopefully, he'll be in a good mood when he gets home.

---

When the door opens, I rush to it, my hands already busying at his coat. He grunts with something like appreciation as I hang it on the hook. His clothes are a little crumpled, as they always are, and he reeks of coffee and cigarettes.

Past that, I remember the early moments, when I was eighteen and he was thirty-nine and his smile promised a whole future. It returns now: a shade of that old expression. "Is that seafood I smell?"

"Yes, it's all laid out. Fresh. Ready to eat... if you are? There's wine too. Chardonnay. I know it sounds funny, but I read online it pairs well with fish."

"It doesn't sound funny," he replies, not unkindly.

But not kind either. It's fine. It's not as if we're going to bridge the gap between us in one night.

We go into the dining room together, and Malcolm grins, rolling up his sleeves. That's the thing in marriages like ours. There are moments of near love between the violence.

He tucks in eagerly, with his hands, tearing apart shells and slurping at the food. I eat slower, and we don't say much. He comments on the food. *It's good*, he tosses that my way, and I know I'll always remember it.

But I have to leave him. He's hurt me too badly. And I'm no saint either.

"How was work?" I ask.

"Same old crap. Doing twice the work for half the pay. They treat me like a slave. You just can't take it out of them. The English in them. The need to oppress."

Why did I bring up work? This side of Malcolm is ugly and relatively new. The spark has drained from him. Maybe I had something to do with that. Since moving to Weston four years ago, he seems to have aged and finally looks old.

"They should appreciate you more. You're the most talented, hardest-working man they've got."

He seems shocked at the compliment. He doesn't deserve it.

"Yeah," he says after a pause. "I am."

"I love you."

He blinks. Stares. I imagine his thoughts, *What is happening here? Why is she trying? We stopped trying a long time ago.*

"I love you too, Lorna."

After dinner, I clean up and Malcolm goes upstairs. He's waiting for me in the bedroom.

I don't enjoy this bit, especially not since we ran from Scotland; a new aspect has entered his sexual side. All the old ills stored up in him, ready to erupt through fist or thrust.

The mattress whines as I envision my hair cut, dyed, fixing whatever problems Sadie has created for herself and then flying into my new life.

"Argh," he groans at the end, a strange, loveless noise, nothing romantic about it.

He rolls aside, falls asleep almost immediately.

I wait until his snores get heavy and then sneak into the en suite, locking the door; he doesn't like that, but I can't risk him catching me. After cleaning myself up, I take the notebook from behind the toilet.

Sadie expects her book of facts. But I can't give her the whole truth. Only surface-level pieces, enough for her to survive. For a little while, at least.

# 8

## SADIE

"You've dyed it the wrong colour."

Lorna has cut her hair into a bob, like mine, but dyed it bleach-blonde instead of my purple. She stares at me from the doorway, my double, and then strides into the room.

"Hello to you too. I can't have *purple* hair. It's too ridiculous. Anyway, you strike me as a woman who changes her hair often."

I shut the door behind her. It takes me a second to work out what's different. "That accent is good."

She grins. "Thank you. Let's hear yours."

I wince, but I've been practising this. "It's not perfect. But I think it will do."

"It's not bad. But you should try to improve it when Malcolm's at work."

She seems far too keen for this, far too confident. I was thinking this morning about the lie I told her, the stuff about my mum, the promise. It's flimsy. My withdrawing brain is sluggish.

She'd have to be intensely naïve for that to have worked, but she doesn't seem that way now. It doesn't matter. She might think her life, her past, is worse than mine. She's wrong.

"So this is it." Lorna drops onto the cheap hotel bed. "We

exchange IDs, walk out of here as different people. Into new lives. Are you sure you want to do this?"

I don't like this. She's acting like she's in charge.

"In your book of facts, do you explain what's so apparently terrible about Malcolm?"

"*Apparently* terrible?" she repeats, folding her arms over a black T-shirt with a vague punky design on it, the sort of thing she imagines I'd wear, I suppose. "You've seen what he does... in public."

"I'm sorry. I didn't mean it like that." I sit next to her, our legs touching. "Does he do more than abuse you? Are there... other things I should be aware of?"

She turns, and I can see myself reflected in her eyes. "The abuse is quite enough. You'll find that out for yourself."

I repress a smile. Okay, if this is true, then this insane plan could work. Malcolm might think he's the big bad wolf, but he's nothing compared to the howls I hear in my dreams. Or the pain which grips me with each bout of morning sickness.

"What about you? What are these *bad things* you mentioned?"

I thought about this last night, how to correct that slip-up. "I wasn't as kind to my mum as I should've been. It's one of the biggest regrets of my life. And I haven't worked as hard as I should have. I was a journalist once, but I've spent the last few years doing basically nothing. Reading books. Living off my inheritance."

"Your inheritance?" Lorna asks sharply.

"It's all gone now. But there's money in my account. Enough."

"Another reason you want to switch?" she taunts.

"I'm doing this to h–"

"Help me, I know. I'm only joking. I'm just so, well, exhilarated. Is that bad? This is the most exciting thing I've ever done."

She must have been playing me yesterday. She's almost giddy

now, her voice teenage-girl-like. So what should I do? Back out? Wait for my past to catch up with me?

"Me too," I say, returning her out-of-place smile.

She's making herself too readable. Or maybe there's something deep inside me, a twin sense, that lets me read her. Was she telling the truth about believing God sent me to her? Perhaps I'm being paranoid.

She's happy to escape her husband, that's all. She's not hiding ugly secrets.

"Sorry if I'm acting weird," Lorna says. "I've been practising being you, and this is how *you* must behave. You're so much more confident than me."

Yes, she's a skilled actress, apparently, slipping into her role with ease. But her role isn't important; she probably won't be performing for long.

"No, it's fine," I say quietly. "And just so you know, my mum wanted to help."

Lorna's eye twitches. I think. For a second but then it's gone, and she's smiling at me innocently. "Pardon?"

"I should've said yesterday. She hired somebody to find you years ago, before your move. Before I had to find you again. . They watched you… like I did, and she wanted to help…"

"So why didn't she?" Lorna says, and I'm almost certain the corner of her lip twitches too.

"She—" What's *wrong* with me? "She was scared. Of Malcolm."

Lorna swallows, her eyes suddenly soft again. When she speaks, it's in my voice, or what she thinks I sound like. "I understand."

I'm wondering if I never should've brought that up to begin with. Maybe I'm making it worse. "How about this for you?" Her accent, her mannerisms, small and defeated. "Is this… close enough?"

Lorna drops the fake accent, narrows her eyes. "Is that how you think I seem to people?"

"I've watched you, remember. It's how you behave around Malcolm."

"Is it?"

I adopt her role again, slightly hunching my shoulders, shrinking myself. I look all over the place, skittish, unable to settle. "Would he be shocked to find this woman waiting for him at home?"

Lorna bites down. Then she stands, shoulders her leather bag, shaking her head. "I can't believe that's really who I've become... no, I don't think he'd be shocked. Excuse me. I need to use the bathroom."

She pushes past me, seeming all fragile again. She's fighting off tears.

# 9

## LORNA

I'm doing a bad thing. But she's really annoyed me. First, with that lazy patch job about her mum, *hired* somebody to look into me, watch Malcolm. Then did nothing, this supposedly angelic woman. But really, it's not about that. It's about what Sadie showed me about myself when she did her impersonation.

She seemed to take too much pleasure in showing me how weak I've become. It was a transformation as impressive as mine. I know where I got my skills of make-believe. What about her?

"Are you okay in there?" she calls.

I sniffle, pretending to fight off another sob. Or maybe I really am. I can't be *this* sensitive. She's the touchy one. But I was almost crying when I ran in here. As I do the bad thing, emotion keeps gripping me.

"F-fine," I say. "I won't be much longer."

Once I'm done, I stand and shoulder my bag. My reflection shows me a new woman, one ready to do whatever she chooses, without a ghoul – Malcolm – following her everywhere.

Sadie's waiting for me just outside the door, wringing her hands. I'm not sure if she's still playing me, or if her nerves are pressing through her confident demeanour. Maybe she knows I was doing something wrong in the bathroom.

"What now?" I ask.

"We become each other. You experience life as a free woman, without worrying about Malcolm."

"And you experience my life. Do you really think you're ready for it?"

She nods in a superior way. It's just how a teacher nods at a child when they've said something silly, like they're going to be prime minister someday. It's a slightly mocking expression; it pushes away any guilt I might feel, after what I've done.

Or the guilt of sending Sadie into my life, letting her overconfidence destroy her.

"What was your mum like?" I ask. I'm curious how much of her story is true. She didn't promise her mum she'd help me; I'm certain of that. It's an insane lie that shows how gullible she thinks I am.

"She was an incredible woman. Dad died when I was young, so she raised me alone. She did a fantastic job. She was so loving, so attentive, more like a sister sometimes. She was my best friend."

I won't let myself feel any jealousy at this… assuming I believe it, which I emphatically do *not*. I won't let myself wish I'd lived her life instead.

"What about our birth parents?" I ask. "Do you know anything about them?"

"Not much. I know our mum was a drug addict. She didn't know who our father was, apparently. After she put us up for adoption, she OD'd. We were better off without her."

When Sadie speaks about our mum being an addict, she stares at the floor. It's easier to read her than most people, which makes sense; it's like reading a reflection. Sadie has had problems with addiction. I'd bet on it. She better keep it under control. Malcolm is a hypocrite when it comes to substances.

"We should try not to contact each other," Sadie goes on. "Obviously, we can if we need to. We've got each other's phone numbers. Speaking of which..."

She takes her mobile from her pocket, handing it to me. When I take it, our hands touch. We stay that way for a short while, looking into each other's eyes, as we contemplate the bizarre journey we're about to embark on.

"This is your chance to tell me anything else I need to know," Sadie says, once I've taken her phone.

I reach into my pocket, and hand her my mobile. "I could say the same to you. Why did you move to Bristol? Why haven't you got a job? Do you have any friends, a partner?"

With each question, she flinches. "It's all in the book," she mutters after a pause. Liar, liar, liar. But I could easily aim that word at myself.

"Same here," I tell her. "So... we're really doing this. I'm Sadie. You're Lorna."

Softening my voice, I approach her, raising my hands to pull her into an embrace. "Thank you so much. Really. You've saved my life. I just hope you haven't forfeited yours."

She squeezes me tightly. "I wish we had more time to get to know each other."

*Why the rush?* I almost ask, but there's no point. She's not going to tell me. Maybe I should ask her if it's because she promised her mother she'd help me by a specific date. Jesus. The bitch didn't even try.

Whatever she's hiding, I'll learn the truth soon enough. And do whatever it takes to protect my new life. "Good luck," I say, once we've exchanged our book of facts.

She still won't look me in the eye. "You too."

---

After leaving the hotel, I wave to Sadie as she walks over to my car. It's the bus for me. Apparently, Sadie rented a car to follow me, but the rental expired yesterday. After checking her address in the book of facts, I use the cash from her purse to buy a bus ticket.

As the bus carries me toward Bristol, I flick through her notebook.

Sadie was born in a village in Lancashire, where she spent her youth disappearing into books and spending time with her mum. She never had many friends, but she didn't need them; she only needed Olivia.

After finishing school, Sadie went to university to study journalism, and then worked for a few years at a small local paper before her mental health got the better of her, and she had to stop working. She lived off her mum's money, and then her inheritance after her mum passed.

And then, she found her mission: found me. It's all too simple and clean.

Her flat is a tiny one-bedroom on the outskirts of Bristol, taking me three buses to reach it. I use the app on her phone – *my* phone – to guide me the final distance.

It's a depressing place. I notice all the differences between my house and hers right away. The silicone sealant along the sink is spotted with black mould. There's damp on the walls. The paint is chipped and faded. There's a stain on the ceiling directly above the oven, oils and fat, a slick, ugly look.

The rest isn't much better. Falling apart, but just about holding it together. Like me, in my old life, before I was free. I decide my first task will be to clean this place up, and then work on fixing the problems I *can* fix.

But first, I sit at the small – tiny, really – table in the corner of the kitchen. I decide to look through her phone, but she's deleted everything: her texts and her call history; her Messenger app. She's deleted everything.

# 10

## SADIE

Wow, wow, wow.

That's all I can think as I pull into the driveway. The garden is large, potted plants ringing the edge of the pristine lawn. I'm used to windows with streaks, blotches of dirt on everything.

Neglect, that's what my world was… before. It's even more impressive inside, with a spacious entranceway, expensive coats hanging from the rack, designer shoes neatly arranged next to the door.

I walk into the kitchen, studying the Aga, the sleek microwave. There's a kitchen island that looks as if it's made from marble, lightning streaks cutting through it.

Lorna's an idiot for giving up this life. No more guilt; no more wondering if I did the right thing. It's over now. Or it soon will be.

My job is to tame the nastier parts of Malcolm. I've got a couple of months before I need to tell him I'm pregnant. Before then, I'll win his trust, show him a new side of Lorna: a side that won't provoke him to hit me.

That's not fair. It's not the victim's fault when the abuser decides to hurt them. But I have to try.

After pouring a cup of orange juice – the brand is one I wouldn't even consider buying in my previous life – I sit in the conservatory, studying her book of facts.

It's all surface-level. Malcolm's favourite colour, his favourite food. The fact that Lorna says grace before every meal; I'll need to remember that.

There's nothing about her life before Weston, except vague comments about living a boring, regular existence in Glasgow. Lorna once worked as a receptionist, but Malcolm convinced her to leave, and now she's a stay-at-home wife, a strange title to me, since it leaves her so much free time to do nothing, to basically waste away.

Whatever. I'll be a stay-at-home *mum* soon, as long as I play this right.

Lorna's clearly hiding something. Or maybe her life really was as dull as the book implies. When I flick the page, I bite down. This is a problem.

*Malcolm doesn't want children. He never has.*

———

When Malcolm returns home, he pauses in the doorway, narrowing his eyes. Fear flutters in me before I remind myself I've dealt with far, far worse.

He looks older up close, the lines around his eyes more pronounced. "Your hair's shorter." He walks right up to me, bringing an odour of sweat and cigarettes.

"Do you like it?" This is the real test: the accent, the lilt of my voice. He could snap at me, *What's wrong with you?* But people see what they want to, and he accepts me as Lorna. I was right when I told Lorna this plan was too crazy for Malcolm to suspect anything.

He stares down at me for a long time. I know this stink in the air, the implication of violence. He's debating hitting me.

But thankfully, he steps away, forces a shaky smile to his face. "It's fine. What's for dinner?"

"I've got a couple of steaks."

I might've gone too far on *steak*, pronouncing it *staaaaaaake*. But again, Malcolm isn't going to assume his wife's twin has replaced her. He just grunts and nods.

"I need a shower."

"Then *I'll* get started on cooking my handsome, wonderful husband a meal."

He tilts his head, then leaves. I guess Lorna doesn't usually compliment him so over-enthusiastically.

Setting the table, I assume Malcolm sits at the head. He returns, wearing jogging bottoms and a hoodie. The brand on the hoodie is another indication of their wealth.

In the book of facts, Lorna told me Malcolm likes his steak well-done. But when he sits, his lip curls. He stabs his fork into the meat and lifts it, staring at me across the table.

"Why didn't you go the whole way and set it on fire?"

Lorna, you lied to me. Shit. "I'm sorry," I whisper, playing the meek wife like I'm trying to win an Oscar.

He scowls. "Get a backbone."

"Do you want mine instead? It's bloody."

He hands me his plate. When I take it, he holds on, a strange sneer creeping across his face, his eyes gleaming like a sadistic child getting ready to inflict pain.

Once we've traded, I clasp my hands together, bow my head. "Dear God, we th–"

Malcolm laughs harshly. "What are you doing?"

"I thought I'd say grace."

"Leave off it. We stopped praying a long time ago. What's wrong with you today?"

Another lie. Why, Lorna?

"Sorry," I mutter again.

"Sorry, sorry," he repeats. "If you were a doll and I pulled your string, that's what you'd say. It's your catchphrase."

He starts aggressively cutting his steak. "Don't forget, my wonderful brother and my even more wonderful sister-in-law are visiting tomorrow."

He lays his fork down. There's meaning in his gaze, but Lorna didn't mention Malcolm's brother in the book. But then again, if she did, it would probably all be fabrications anyway.

"I want you on your best behaviour. You know what Rory's like, but that's no excuse. I never…"

"What?" I whisper, because I have to learn as much as possible.

But I can't ask for more information, because Lorna would already know.

"I never enjoy hurting you," he says, then shoves a big bloody piece of steak into his mouth.

# 11

## LORNA

Cleaning the flat brings me a sense of peace. The chemicals wash away any doubt, as I scrub the mould from the silicone sealant around the sink. The oven is disgusting, but two hours of hard work has it gleaming.

It's nice to be able to hum as I work, not having to worry about Malcolm snapping at me to shut up. I wonder how Sadie's first evening is going. She's learned what I did in the hotel bathroom by now: adding lies to the book of facts. It was petulant, maybe, and part of me wishes I could take it back.

But it's done now. Sitting in the living room – I've dusted and hoovered, but there's still a stale smell to the place – I go through Sadie's purse. She has a driver's licence and some cash, and there's a note in here too…

*The back of the bottom-left kitchen drawer.*

Sadie clearly loves leaving me notes. It's like she has a fetish for it. In the back of the drawer, I find the rest of the cash, enough so I don't have to work for three or so months. I also find the lease for the flat. Sadie has already paid five months upfront, which seems odd to me.

That's not what landlords usually ask for, is it? But if her credit is bad… and if she doesn't have good references… She doesn't have a laptop or a computer. The flat is stunningly bare, in fact, no books or photos or any indicators about who Sadie really is.

I wish I could ignore it, simply push on with this new reality. But what happens if her dark past catches up to me?

*I've done some bad things…*

That's what she said.

I download the Kindle app on her phone, then browse the catalogue. I almost want to pick something thrilling, but I settle on a fantasy romance. I used to read these books often as a girl, princesses and princes, clichés and bullshit. I go into the bedroom.

Lying on the thin mattress, with somebody blasting music from the next flat – the walls are paper-thin – I lose myself in the book. I rarely read anymore, since I'm always on edge, either thinking about the last time Malcolm *disciplined* me or anticipating the next time he will.

But now, despite the noise, despite the filth, I'm able to disappear into the story. Until Sadie's phone rings. *My* phone. This is going to take some getting used to.

The number is unknown, but that doesn't mean Sadie doesn't know the caller. She deleted her call history and her contacts for a reason. It's tempting to run. But I want to make this life work.

I have to face whatever this is.

"So you've finally seen sense," a gruff voice says when I answer. "I've only rung you about ten thousand bloody times."

"I'm sorry," I say, remembering to make my accent English.

It turns out all that practise with Dad has finally become worthwhile. Not that I enjoyed it, even for a second. But it shaped me… I can't look back on that time. On all the mistakes. They don't belong to me anymore.

"If you're sorry, come home."

"I can't do that."

"At least let me see you. Talk to you. I know you're in Bristol."

I sit up. "How do you know that?"

"I heard it on the grapevine, darling. A woman with dyed hair, shifty as hell, roamed the streets of Bristol one night looking for a fix. But just as you were about to finish the deal, you panicked. You ran. We've got feelers everywhere. You should know that by now."

So I was right. Sadie's into drugs.

Does she owe this man money?

"Fine," I say. "We can meet. But it has to be in public."

"R-really?"

"Isn't that what you want?"

"I didn't expect you to agree."

"I'm tired of running. I don't want to have to look over my shoulder for the rest of my life."

"All right. How does tomorrow work?"

"Tomorrow works fine."

*What's your name? Who are you? Why are you chasing me?* Or, really, why is he chasing Sadie?

"I'll text you a café and a time," I say.

"You're not going to pull some stunt, are you? You're agreeing to this way too easily."

Because I need answers.

"I want to fix this," I say. "Then I can move on."

"Move on? Is that how you think this ends?"

"If you're going to try and bully me over the phone, I'm cancelling."

"No, no. I'm sorry. I didn't mean that. It's just... I want you to come home. We all do."

"We'll talk about it tomorrow."

I hang up, then take a few slow breaths. Whatever I have to do to make this man – and his friends, the *we* he mentioned – back off – I'll do it. I wasn't always a broken thing.

# 12

## SADIE

Malcolm seems more interested in me when we go to bed. He's got a pawing, pouting attitude I've encountered before.

He tugs at my clothes like I'm a mannequin he needs to undress. I keep playing meek, even if it goes against my instincts. Thankfully, he keeps the lights off, basically dragging me to bed, and then grunting a few times; it's like I'm not even here.

As he groans toward his end, I feel it: the itch for a fix. It's easier to distance myself with the juice in my veins. But what Malcolm does is nothing compared to what I've survived before.

And then he rolls over, starts snoring almost right away. I stare at the ceiling for a long time. I've endured harsher punishment than this.

In the morning, I rise early, before Malcolm. Going downstairs, I sit in the conservatory with the door open, smelling the flowers from the garden – a fenced green with beds all along the sides: everything in its place – and savouring the cool morning feeling.

When I hear Malcolm getting up, I make him some coffee. Lorna's book of facts tells me he has an espresso in the morning.

Judging from Malcolm's grunt of approval, it seems she told the truth about something, at least.

"I'll be meeting Rory and Skye after work. We'll all come home together."

"What time?" I ask, remembering his warning from last night.

*You know what Rory's like, but that's no excuse.*

"I'll have some dinner ready."

"I'll text you," he grunts. "I need to shower. Long day of doing all the work and getting half the credit. I hate England."

"Me too," I say, my accent not *quite* right, but passable.

I've got an advantage; apart from a few words and his physical demands, Malcolm pays hardly any attention to his wife. He doesn't even look at me as we speak, like he can't stand the sight of me: of Lorna.

He makes for the hallway, then pauses, turns back. His dressing gown is open in the middle, showing the grey-black hairs spread across his chest. It's disgusting, really. "It might be time to open the box soon."

*The box?*

I hold the words back. Lorna would know what this box is, though she didn't mention it in her book. It's clear she didn't mention *anything* that was actually important.

Even if I did the same, I resent the bitch for it.

"Do you want me to bring it…"

*Down? Up?*

"In here, for later?"

I yell when he surges across the room. I didn't know he could move that fast. The noise I make is an instinct, but I quickly kill it. Malcolm has kindly wrapped his hand around my throat to help in the silence. He's stronger than he looks.

I raise my hands, meaning to fight, but then he narrows his eyes in a tell-tale way. Lorna wouldn't fight; he's not used to her raising her hands. Jesus, how pathetic. If he tries to hit me in the belly…

I'll have to hurt him. Badly. Then what?

He leans close, breathing his hot, ugly breath all over me. "Why are you so keen all of a sudden?"

I grab his wrist, wishing I could kill this man. "Puh-please." I gasp. "M-M-Malcolm."

He lets go, curling his lip. "Don't pretend like you want to open the box. It's not fair."

"I think your opinion matters too," I say vaguely, the safest option, and one that will hopefully give my raw neck some time to recover. My voice is raspy.

"Seriously, are you joking?"

He's speaking as if he didn't just choke me. But that's the casual tone the abuse in this marriage has taken. I need to figure out a way to make it stop. Could I kill? I essentially sent Lorna to her death. They're fiercer than Malcolm could ever be.

"I want to make you happy."

"Hmm," he says, turning away. "I'll think about it. The box is always fun. But you told me you never wanted to do it again. A new life, remember?"

*Do what again, you abusive monster.*

"I care about you, Malcolm."

He smirks, then leaves me to massage my burning throat, as I wonder what I've just started.

# BAD, VIOLENT, TEARFUL

You talked about being a parent once.

They were the idealistic words of a bright-eyed youth, staring up at the sky as if you'd only just discovered its existence. You were longing and smiling, and you said, "I think I could do it. Raise a child. Do right by them."

I'm not proud of what I said in reply. It was something unnecessarily cruel. I used to be like that, spitting vitriol for the sake of it. Or, truthfully, for what I mentioned before: the indulgent succulent nature of pain for some people. For me. It felt good.

By the end of it – it was bad, violent, tearful – you were telling me you never wanted to be a parent. You were saying I'd ruined that for you, because of my nature. You said you just wanted the world to burn. You'd had enough. Nothing was fair. Everything was going to hell anyway.

"End it, then, end it."

Another time, a knife held to your throat, crying and begging for me to kill you. The demons in your mind were staring at you, as I stood there, and the knife tasted better.

A drop of blood slid down your neck and then you crumpled,

sagged to the floor, weeping as the knife clattered onto the hardwood.

I was the one to comfort you. You held onto me so tight.

It's a vicious and interesting aspect of human nature, how the victim will often sprint into the so-called solace of the demon's arms. My arms. I'm not a demon. I'm a human being just like you, only attuned differently to the nature of the world. Responsive to different things.

I think you would have – or still could – make an excellent parent. If you managed to keep the ugly parts of yourself tucked away.

# 13

## LORNA

I walk into the café, projecting the sort of powerful energy I let go of a long time ago. Head held high, dignity and fierceness etched into my features, I look around the dingy space.

It's a small area, tucked in between a used electronics store and a butchers. A teenage girl stands behind a counter drumming her fingernails against it.

A man stands as I enter. He's tall and lean, sharp cheekbones, wearing a full grey tracksuit with one of those man bags slung across his front. He's a few years older than me, his thinning hair peeled back and glistening with all the hair product he's wearing.

At least I don't have to guess who I'm here to meet. He rushes over, then stops when I take a step back. "I'm not going to hurt you," he says, voice gruff, a heavy London accent. "Do you want a coffee?"

"Sure."

He gestures at a table. As I sit, he goes to the counter and orders me a drink.

"Your favourite," he says with a small smile, laying the mug down.

It's a latte, and it really is my coffee of choice. That's not a world-shattering coincidence. Sadie and I have the same taste-buds.

"I guess I should get right down to it," he says.

How do I learn this man's name without outright asking? Which is something I can't do, since Sadie would already know.

"Your hair looks nice, by the way."

"I thought you wanted to get right down to it."

He flinches. "Fair enough. We want you to come home."

"Why?" And who is *we*?

"Don't get clever. You know why we need you back."

"Maybe I want you to say it," I snap, deciding anger is my best route.

And it's not all forced. I'm supposed to be starting my new life, and now I've got to clean up whatever mess Sadie has made. It's not fair. But I knew this was going to be more complicated than her 'Mummy made me do it' lie implied.

"Maybe I'm ready to move on," I say, when he doesn't respond.

He slams his hand on the table. "If *you* want to move on, all right, fair enough, but you can't steal our child."

My hand goes to my belly. Sadie's pregnant? I picture Malcolm's face when he finds out.

The man follows my hand with his gaze, nodding tightly. "You look great, by the way, and not just your hair. Healthier. Sobriety agrees with you."

"I had no choice," I say, thinking quickly. "I couldn't inflict that on our child."

He leans closer, lowering his voice. "George said nobody's heard from you. You haven't been answering our phone calls. I was shocked when you picked up for me. You need to let us do a paternity test, at least. You don't even know who the father is."

Oh, Sadie, you naughty girl. But I'm not sure it's quite as simple as Sadie sleeping with multiple men. There's darkness in this man's eyes, a hint of guilt too.

"The kid could be mine. Or George's. Or Benny's. Or Toby's."
With each name, his tone gets bleaker.

"I was thinking, if you're the father, we should name him after you."

He laughs humourlessly. "Jonesy Junior. It has a nice ring to it." There: a name, a tiny piece of information.

"That night," he goes on. "It wasn't supposed to be like that. I never wanted to hurt anybody. But you played your part too. You know you did."

I take a long sip of coffee, ignoring the heat, biding my time. I don't like the way he's looking at me at all; it reminds me of Malcolm. He's not seeing a person. He's seeing meat.

"What if I don't want to do a paternity test? What if I want to stay here, and live my life in peace?"

"Then you're shit out of luck. Because I'm not going anywhere."

"What about the others? Have you told them you're here?"

He shakes his head slowly. "If I told George, things could get nasty. I don't want that. I never did. But if you keep messing us around, I'll have no choice. George will come down here... do you think he'll be happy when he sees you?"

So this man came here alone. I don't like being threatened. Reaching across the table, I compose myself. I'm good at hiding my feelings. When I touch his hand, he looks almost boyish. He squeezes mine with surprising gentleness.

"I've got a lot to do today," I tell him. "But I'd like to spend some proper time with you. We can *really* talk things over... in private. At my flat."

"Don't mess me around. What have you got to do that's so important?"

"Job interviews. And I'm meeting somebody about a car. I'm trying to build a life. Just give me some time. I've missed you."

Jonesy wraps both his hands around mine, looking at me with clear implication. "If you disappear, I'll call the others. George will turn this city over to find you. It'll take time, but we'll do it. And then…"

He doesn't have to say more.

"I promise," I say, withdrawing my hand. "Tomorrow."

He nods, no clue what the woman sitting opposite him is capable of.

# 14

## SADIE

Somehow, I've burned the roast potatoes. And the chicken is dry. Malcolm texted that he wanted a midweek roast for when Rory and Skye arrived. Clearly, I've got to do what the bully says.

The little prick. I'd love to stamp on his head.

My throat is still raw from where he grabbed me, my body aching in other places too from last night. But at least he didn't touch my belly. I rush around the kitchen, but there's no way to salvage the potatoes. They're charred and blackened.

*You can live your life in imagination*, Mum used to tell me. *All you have to do is will it.*

That's the problem; I've been daydreaming about seriously hurting Malcolm after what he did to me, distracting from the cooking. I don't know how Lorna tolerated him for so long.

He'll be easier to manage than Jonesy and George and the others, those sick freaks. How can you do what they did and still call yourself a human being?

And there's *the box*, whatever that is.

I've spent the day searching the house, but there was nothing apart from bills and old photos. Lorna doesn't have social media.

In her book of facts, she gave me the password to her laptop, but there's nothing on there apart from yoga workout music, solitaire, the usual stuff.

She's hiding something. Nobody is this boring.

"What's that bloody smell?"

I turn – too late, no time left. My heartbeat is pounding like I'm a character in a goddamned book.

Malcolm stands in the doorway, scowling. At his side, a taller, fatter, uglier man stands, with a flat red face and a giant forehead. He's leering at me, eyes glistening in a way that reminds me of my life before: the things I'd do to make the withdrawals withdraw.

A woman stands at his other shoulder, dainty, clasping her hands together like a Victorian lady. She looks like she hates me too, brushing her grey hair from her face, properly glaring. They're at least twenty years older than me, nearer to Malcolm's age.

"Is it edible?" Rory says, walking over and looking down at the chicken. "It doesn't look edible, Malc."

"Leave her alone." Skye joins us, no hellos, no *how have you been*. She glances at the chicken, then at Malcolm. "But he's right, I'm afraid."

Malcolm sighs. "Fuck it. I'll get us pizza."

"And waste all this food?" I say.

Rory laughs meanly. There's nothing kind in this man at all. I've spent enough time around bad men to know one when I see one. "Sweet Lorna, you can carry it down to the hobo house if you like. But for me – I'll take a meat feast, Malc."

"A small vegetable for me," Skye says.

"Right."

Without asking what I want, Malcolm turns and strides away, stamping his feet. I think about hurting him again.

They're really going to throw away this food. The potatoes, fine, but the tough chicken *is* edible, just not perfectly cooked.

The people from my life before would've devoured it. If they could summon an appetite.

"How's England treating you?" Rory says, idly toying with the metal handle of a knife in the block.

There's an air of a threat about it. Like he wants me to think the worst. "Fine. Quiet."

"Yoga and reading and anything but work, hmm?" Skye has walked right up to me, standing so close I can smell her perfume. I can't turn without giving Rory my back, and I'll look paranoid if I shimmy off to the side to keep both of them in view. "I haven't been satisfying Rory."

Before I can react to this bizarre statement, Rory nods matter-of-factly. "It's true."

"It's a shame," Skye goes on. "But I'm not the woman I was."

Rory scoffs, slipping the knife from the block with a *rasp* sound. "You can say that again."

I stiffen, thinking of cold metal and blooming blood and losing the only thing which has ever mattered to me. The life growing inside.

"I'm old and disgusting. I'm far too thin. And oh, Lorna, my vagina is a *mess.*"

"A *mess,*" Rory repeats in disgust.

They speak so casually, as though this is completely regular, as though they don't expect Lorna – me – to react. I walk to the sink, letting me put some distance between us at least. Pouring a glass of water, I say, "Would you like a drink?"

"What we'd like is your help," Skye replies. "I can't satisfy my poor husband. It's not fair. I'm an ugly, ancient skeleton. There's nothing appealing about me whatsoever."

Rory laughs harshly. "Disgusting bitch."

My hand shakes as I take a sip of water. I almost choke on it.

"I don't think you're ugly," I say.

"Look at this." Skye grabs the skin of her neck, tugging at it so harshly it turns red. "I'm a fucking turkey."

"She's revolting, Lorna. Let's not pretend."

Rory moves with the same surprising speed as his brother. Skye laughs like a sadist as he surges across the kitchen, stopping right in front of me, the sharp expensive knife in his hand. This is it. They're going to force me to... I can't even think about it. Pathetically, I'm close to crying. My belly throbs as I stare at the knife.

"You should carve the chicken." He gently trails the tip of my blade across the back of my hand, as though it's ordinary, grinning as he does it. "You can make sandwiches with the meat, at least."

I take the knife. Our hands touch, and he seems to like it. Behind him, Skye laughs again. She sounds ill.

"Easy, tiger," Rory says, then finally returns to his wife.

I carry the knife to the tray, shaking all over, not sure what to do.

# 15

## LORNA

He's still standing outside my flat, in the light of the lamp-post. It's the man from the café, Jonesy, the possible father to Sadie's unborn child. The junkie who chased her to Bristol.

Sadie's flat – *my* flat – is on a hill, near a derelict mental asylum, a relic from the old days.

He should take it as a sign. There be madwomen about.

I'm still debating going out there. Since meeting him earlier today, I've spent the afternoon trying to figure out how to handle this. And trying *not* to give in to the anger swirling inside of me. A maelstrom of fire, really, even if that sounds melodramatic.

He can't take this from me. No more Malcolm. No more box. No more memories. I'll wipe them away, create a new version of Sadie, one who'd never associate with scum like Jonesy.

Screw it.

Pulling on Sadie's tattered punky boots, I quickly walk downstairs, pushing onto the small untidy courtyard area. A woman in her fifties leaps back, out of my way. I'm coming like a missile.

"Sorry," I say.

She smiles, shaking her head. She's got a steady look about her, her dark, grey-brown hair tied up in a ponytail. She's wearing hiking boots and cargo trousers and a shirt with her sleeves rolled up, big chunky garden gloves.

"No harm done," she says. "Where are you going in such a hurry?"

"To see a friend."

"You're new here, aren't you?"

"Yes. I don't think I've seen you before, either."

"I'm Elizabeth," she says. "Sorry about that. I'm so skittish sometimes. Scatter-brained too. What's *your* name?"

There's something kind about her, inviting. I've never had many friends. I'm too scared usually. Of who I am, of who they might be. But not anymore. If I'm going to make a change, I have to try.

"Sadie," I tell her.

"Thought I'd clear this place up," Elizabeth says, gesturing at the courtyard. "Somebody has to. Go on now, on your way. I won't keep you. But it *was* nice to see you. You're the friendliest face in the whole building."

I grin. It feels good. "I don't think so, Elizabeth. That's you."

It's a small moment, but it means a lot.

"I'm flat twenty-one, by the way, if you ever need me."

"Thanks so much," I reply. "I'm number nine. I should warn you, though, I haven't got any decent biscuits."

That makes her smile, and I feel a little better about myself. Maybe this version of me doesn't have to be so shy all the time.

I leave her, opening the creaky gate and turning to the end of the road, then turning again so I'm on my flat's side. Jonesy is leaning against the wall under the lamp-post, not even trying to hide the fact he's following me.

"May I ask why you're lurking outside my flat like a serial killer?"

He laughs humourlessly, fiddling with his man bag. "I was always going to follow you. You must've known that. I can't have you disappearing on me again. And anyway, *you're* supposed to be busy."

I clench my jaw, thinking of the items I purchased earlier. A Stanley knife and a hammer. Other things, too. But it won't come to that. I hope.

"What's your plan? Stand out here all night?"

"If I have to."

"I could still sneak out of the flat. You can only see the kitchen from here. I could just walk out the main door."

"Yeah, I guess that's a good point. Thanks for the tip. Maybe I was hoping you'd take pity on me. Invite me inside. I've missed you."

Men. They think they can do anything they want, take everything from a person. Turn her to meat. Turn her into the punchline of a violent joke. Jonesy is no better.

"I'll invite you in…" He tenses with anticipation. He's truly pitiful. "But first, you have to say what happened that night."

"Why? You were there."

"But you have to *say* it."

I infuse my voice with all the righteous rage of a wronged woman. It's not difficult.

"You were involved. You can't hide from it. Say it, Jonesy. You owe me that much."

He stuffs his hands in his pockets, bowing his head. "This is stupid."

"Then stay here. I don't care."

"Fine, Jesus… We were at George's. We were all drunk and high. You were the only woman. You started getting frisky with George, and then George asked if you'd like to do us all. You said yes. It was a good time, lots of fun. *You* had fun. You did. Nobody's that good at acting."

I am, you sick bastard. Sadie had *fun*? No woman would pass herself around to a bunch of lowlifes like Jonesy for enjoyment. Drugs, or maybe she was forced.

Those men will come here if I don't give Jonesy what he wants. Which I can't do; I'm not returning to that sad existence.

"Let's go upstairs," I say. "I'll make you a cup of coffee."

I just wish I had some poison.

# 16

## SADIE

"So how is the yoga going?" Skye asks, daintily cutting into her pizza with a knife and fork. She doesn't seem at all like the woman who shared intimate details of her sex life, who giggled madly as her husband intimidated me.

Rory grins. "It keeps her young. Not that she *needs* to be kept young. We're the dinosaurs, aren't we, Malc?"

"Yeah," Malcolm grunts, then stuffs a pizza slice into his mouth.

The food doesn't match the surroundings of the dining room, the large gold-framed mirror, the miniature chandelier. Selling this table could keep a junkie soaring for a week at least.

"It's going well, thank you," I say.

My only choice is to follow them: play the civilised game, pretend none of that other stuff happened. I can still feel the knife trailing across the back of my hand, the cold metal point.

"How often do you do it?"

"All day, every bloody day," Malcolm says.

"You must get bored down here, Lorna," Skye says. "No friends. No other... interests."

I'm watching everybody carefully. I have to. It's a way to fight back. I've had to take so much in my life, tolerate all kinds of crap since I made the stupid choice to slip that needle into my arm and taste its sweet release.

Everybody tightens at the word *interests*.

"Are you going to ruin dinner?" Malcolm says, staring at his brother, as if he thinks he has the ability to instantly shut his wife up. There's a familiar bullyish glint in his eyes.

Rory shrinks in his chair, as if his big brother is melting him. "No, of course not."

Something just happened: an allusion. *Interests*.

"Are we making you nervous, sister-in-law?" Rory says, no clue he sounds like a cheesy baddie in a film. The *wanker*. I hate him for scaring me. "You've barely touched your food."

"I'm fine," I tell him, looking down at my chicken sandwich. Upon gracefully returning with the pizza, my loving husband grunted, nodded to the kitchen, no pizza for me. My punishment for ruining dinner.

"So what *do* you do?" Skye asks.

"I read. I do yoga. I keep the house clean. I care for my husband. It's a simple life, but I'm proud of it."

"Well said," Malcolm mumbles.

I experience a small version of something which must've been familiar to Lorna. A thrill of pride when Malcolm tosses anything good in his wife's direction. As if she, as if *I* should be grateful for kindness instead of a fist.

"So... Malc." Rory clears his throat. "How's work? These English bastards still looking out for each other, eh?" The *eh* sounds so desperate, but then Malcolm begins ranting about work, basically shouting between starving-man mouthfuls of pizza. He obviously enjoys ranting about this topic. It seems like Rory's way of saying sorry.

As he speaks, I look around the beautiful dining room. There are so many kind, hard-working, honest people who will never sit in a room like this. It has a grandfather clock, for Christ's sake. It looks like an antique piece, ticking away. Further down, at the base…

I'm tempted to lean closer, but Malcolm looks at me, saying something. I agree, *yes, dear*, and that's good enough for him. He doesn't see me. He doesn't care.

Something is sticking out from the base of the clock. It looks like the corner of a notebook. Or maybe it's just a piece of rubbish. But it's too square, a pale blue colour, the very edge of it. I didn't search under there today when I made my circuit of the house.

"Anyway," Malcolm says, once his ranting has shuddered to a stop. "I need to take a piss. Try to entertain yourselves while I'm gone."

Malcolm leaves, and I have to stop thinking about the grandfather clock. Or what might be written in that notebook. If it *is* a notebook.

Rory rests his elbows on the table, leering at me. Skye has her sadist's face on. They become different people the second we're alone. "You're going to be good for us when Malcolm's at work tomorrow, aren't you, Lornie?"

"Little Lornie," Skye whispers, with a sickening emphasis on the *little*, trailing her fingernail up and down her neck, the same place she grabbed before. It's still a little red. "I've brought your favourite toys."

"I don't want that," I say, the simplest and vaguest refusal I can think of.

They exchange a look. Skye titters. Rory grins meanly. "We don't want to ruin your life, my little Lornie. We don't want to post photos through your neighbours' letter boxes. You know what photos I'm talking about, don't you?"

I can guess. What did Lorna get herself into? After I nod, Rory claps his hands together. "Right, that's sorted then."

"What's sorted?" Malcolm says, walking into the room.

"Lorna's going to teach Skye some yoga tomorrow. My poor wife, she's beginning to suffer from mobility issues."

# 17

## LORNA

"This is a nice place," Jonesy says, looking around the ugly flat.

I've cleaned, it's true. No more grimy dishes or stains on the surfaces. But everything is still old and worn. But this is useful information; it means my flat is nicer than the sorts of places Jonesy, Sadie, and all their friends usually stay.

"Thanks. Would you like a drink?"

He grins, stuffing his hands in his pockets. "When did you get so polite? A cuppa, if it's going. Two sugars."

I walk the short distance to the kitchen. Jonesy paces in the living room with heavy footsteps, ownership steps, the kind designed to let a woman know just how worthless she is.

"So where's your stash?" he calls.

"I don't have one. I'm done with it."

"Goddamn." He pauses at the threshold, watching me make the teas. From where he's standing, he could see the plastic bag on the counter: the one with the Stanley knife in. "Cold turkey?"

"Yes."

"That's suicidal."

"I did it anyway."

"For the baby?"

"Yes."

Perhaps this is true, Sadie courageously charging at her sobriety, doing whatever it takes. Or maybe she's sneakily slipping pills and the odd injection, despite her pregnancy. I don't know and can't afford to care.

"You know I tried to calm things down."

"I'm sorry?"

He shifts on the spot. "Back there, before you left, with George and that lot... I told them to take it easy. You remember that, don't you?"

He's fishing. Ah, here it is. I read his face. His hideous, stupid expression. My father would've called him a prize pig: a prime mark.

"I remember everything," I tell him coldly.

It gets me the response I want. He steps back, fists clenched, eyes all panicky. He did something evil that night. Let's say it like it is. Plain speech. They gang-raped my twin.

Be a slut, be a loving wife, be a doting mother, be a silent nothing. A man's voice twitches, a woman's bones break.

"Two sugars, you said?"

"Yeah."

He returns to the living room before me, giving me a chance to grab the Stanley knife and slip it into my pocket. We sit at the small glass coffee table, across from each other. There's a piece of tape stuck to it that won't budge no matter how much I pick at it.

"I thought you were pretty out of it that night."

"I was, but I felt weirdly aware. I remember every single detail."

I've arranged the knife specifically so I can slip my hand in, grab it, and then slide the mechanism as I withdraw it. Then what? Reality, bleeding. Seeping violence. Does part of me want it?

If Sadie and I are the same, I wonder why she never awoke this piece of herself. Ourselves.

"So you remember me trying to calm them down, then?"

"I remember you joining in," I reply.

"But at the end. When they were getting really bad."

"You might have said a couple of words."

"I *did.*" He's trying to convince himself. "I never wanted to use you. I loved you once. I think I still do. I never wanted you to become... you know, what you have, with George and that."

"A whore to be passed around? A dirty skank waiting for her next needle?"

I've hit the truth. He looks away guiltily. "I'd never call you that."

"But that's what I was..."

Oh, Sadie, what a mess. "But not anymore," I go on. "We might as well get this over with. I want you to leave, go back, tell George you couldn't find me. Tell him you spoke to some men who told you I'd left the country. Whatever. I never want to see *any* of you again."

He's already shaking his head before I've finished talking. "That's not an option."

"I'm not coming home."

He shrugs. "Then I'll have to tell George you're here."

Okay, Jonesy. If this is how you want to play it. Using the practice I gained from my dad, and then from Malcolm, I change my shape. I become a werewolf, but a beautiful one, rising to my feet and turning my head just so, and Jonesy can't help it. I activate the animal in him.

Idiot. That's exactly what he's done to me. Woken the beast. There's a drumbeat deep inside. This isn't for Dad. It's not for Malcolm. It has nothing to do with the box. This is all for me.

"At least give me tonight," I say, as I stride across the room, all hips and eyes. "Who knows what could happen by morning?"

His mind goes straight to sex. What a surprise. Mine goes

somewhere darker. Reality is threatening to bleed. And I'm tempted to let it.

# 18

## SADIE

"The dinner wasn't too bad, was it?" I whisper, cuddling up to Malcolm in bed.

He's a warm body, even if I hate him, hate the necessity for this. There's a more important warmth, the one inside me, the life growing. My future. My chance to make something of myself.

Mum always wanted grandkids. Well, Olivia did, my adopted mother. Not our birth mum.

Malcolm squeezes my shoulder, breathing in a somehow grumbling manner. I haven't had a chance to check the grandfather clock yet: the hidden *something*.

"It was fine," he says.

"Rory wasn't... *too* bad."

I need to know what Malcolm meant when he said I know what his little brother is like. Does Malcolm know about their weird sexual stuff? The blackmail? The threats?

"He's a wanker. He's lucky I even let him visit."

"Why do you?"

Malcolm's fist tightens on my shoulder. "Don't ask stupid questions."

"Sorry," I say quickly, thinking of a thousand different ways to kill this man. And wondering where Rory's apparent power originates from. He's got a hold over Malcolm, it seems, something that forces Malcolm to tolerate him within reason. Until Rory pushes him too far.

"He won't be here long," my twin's oh-so loving husband goes on. "I don't like the way he looks at you. He thinks I don't see it, but he's attracted to you. He always has been."

"What would you do if he ever tried anything?" I murmur, the back of my hand tingling as though Rory's dragging the knife across it again.

"With you? Are you trying to start a fight?"

"No." I snuggle closer, ignoring every instinct I have, and gently smooth my hand across his chest. I kiss his sweaty stinky shoulder. "I'm just curious."

"I'd kill him," Malcolm grunts. "Now go to sleep."

He rolls over, leaving me to shimmy to the edge of the bed. This is where I'll stay, waiting, until he falls asleep.

If Malcolm would kill Rory for trying anything with me, that means he can't know about the bizarre insinuations. I've been around enough freaks to know Rory and Skye have got some co-dependent sadistic tendencies. I remember how Skye laughed when he launched himself at me.

And the threat. The photos. Malcolm doesn't know about any of it. Lorna has screwed me. Soon, Malcolm begins to snore.

I rise from the bed, moving slowly, remembering times where I crept across crack houses to steal cigarettes, tiptoeing over unconscious bodies. They didn't seem human as I held my arms out to the side, balancing myself, still a little high, but also angry that I'd have to get more again soon.

Down the stairs, I stalk to the dining room. I can't let myself worry about what happens if Malcolm wakes up. Or Rory. Or even Skye, the sick bitch.

Slipping into the dining room, I leave the light off, letting the moonlight shine through the window. The floor is cool against my knees. My back twinges, my body aching, but that's nothing new. Aches and pains are a junkie's life.

And soon, my back will have to support a baby. That's why I'm doing this. That's why I need the truth.

I grab the corner of the blue object, pull. It *is* a notebook, the paper curled at the edges. I try to open the main section of the clock, but there's a keyhole, and I didn't find a key during my search.

Malcolm must have it. Standing, I open the book. Read part of the first line.

*I've always done whatever I have to do. My father taught me that. But he would come to regret it.*

Are these Lorna's words?

I panic when the door begins to whine open. Fall to my knees so hard a jolt smashes through my legs, into my belly, and suddenly I'm convinced I've just murdered my child with the sudden movement.

Quickly replacing the notebook, I look up to find Malcolm staring down, hands behind his back.

"Why are you on the floor?" His eyes flit to the grandfather clock, and he grins. "Are you looking for something, dear wife? You don't have the key."

He steps forward, his big belly catching the steel-blue light, his grin widening. "Are you that desperate for the box?"

I've got no choice but to stand when he offers his hand. If he goes for me, I'll need to protect my belly. Turn my back, give him my face, my arms, whatever it takes.

I shudder when he pulls me into an embrace. "You *know* you don't have the key."

Does this mean he doesn't know about the journal? Too many damn questions.

"I thought you might've left it unlocked," I murmur. "I'm sorry. It was stupid. *I'm* stupid."

"Hush," he whispers, gently kissing the top of my head. A

game or a trick before the violence; or a brief flash of love to convince himself he's not a monster. "You're not stupid for finding this life dull. You'd be stupid if you didn't. But you have to be sure. You need to fully commit. Can you do that?"

*No.* Not yet. Not until I know what I'm agreeing to. Risking a fist, I whisper, "Oh, God, I'm not sure."

He ends the hug, turns away. "Then stop wasting my bloody time. And get back to bed."

The journal will have to wait until tomorrow. *He would come to regret it.* What, Lorna, what would your father come to regret?

# 19

## LORNA

You always were a bad child. There's something wrong with you. You're not even here, are you? Where do you go, Lorna? Where do you fly away to?

I'm hissing and spitting and plunging my hand deep, barely aware of it except for the heat and the thickness of the blood. It's not my fault.

It's his, for doing things to women, to my sister: for implying he'd do the same to me. To be so willing to participate in an assault and then try to convince the victim he's on *her* side.

Over and over, I move the blade, as his clawing hands get limper at my shoulders. I'm almost back in reality. I almost slip, nearly collapse into myself, but I manage to stay away, until even the warmth of the blood recedes. I'm not doing this.

I'm not here. It's all over now anyway.

Closing my eyes, I fall away from the messy lump, collapse into memories of such violence I can't even acknowledge the details. It's like an abattoir in some of them, chains and hanging meat, and the stink of death, the stink of all the wrong things a person can do.

A gleaming smile. *You did good.* Now, as the fire fades, the rage dies, I know I'll regret this.

"Puh-please," Jonesy whispers.

He's crying and his hands paw weakly at the lacerated ruin of his belly. "I'm sorry," I say, then finish the job.

# BURSTING BRIGHTNESS

Sometimes, I black out. I can't help it.

There's this sudden flash, usually of emotion, but I see it too. A bursting brightness like I'm glimpsing heaven. And then I come back to myself, and whatever's done, is done. I don't like it. I prefer to be in control.

It's not fair, life, the nature of oneself. You know that better than anybody.

You've tried so hard to improve on yourself. You bury all your nastiest secrets in a box in the back of your mind. Everybody does that. It would be impossible to stay sane otherwise. There's only so much a person can take.

But you need to understand that they can't stay buried forever. That's what you've always fucking got wrong. I'm sorry for swearing, but Jesus, it's the truth. Bad things happen when people forget who they are.

Husbands rape. Sisters lie. Killers hide in plain sight. But I've never, not for a single moment, forgotten who *I* am.

# 20

## SADIE

Malcolm moved the journal. Dammit. I'm on my hands and knees in the dining room, reaching underneath the clock, my arm aching. I'm so sick of the junkie pain, my body screaming out for a release, just one, enough to wash away the temptation.

And then what? My baby comes out with two bloody heads. *No.*

"What are you doing, little Lornie?"

I look up to find Rory swaggering into the room. He's wearing a dressing gown over the top of stripy pyjamas, holding a steaming mug of coffee. He looks so much less threatening than George and the others, it's laughable.

Whatever this is, I can handle it. But what about the journal? Malcolm knows that's why I was down there. He's going to be angry when he gets home. Unless it wasn't him who moved it?

"Cleaning."

"Hmm." Rory taps his fingernail against his mug. "If you say so. Or maybe you thought I hid the photos down there. You know the ones."

I roll my eyes. So we're starting right away this morning.

"Well done, Rory. You've found a way to exploit my naked body. What a clever, clever man you are."

This is a risk, but it pays off. Rory's grin widens, telling me I'm right. "Or maybe I'll go and talk with the neighbours about Faraday Cottage, eh? Would you prefer that?"

There's no way for me to ask what happened at the cottage. I'm supposed to already know. He's staring with lethal implication in his cruel eyes; whatever it is, it has power over Lorna, over me.

It might be time to ring her soon. If she's still around. What if George and the others have found her already?

"That's what I thought," Rory says in response to my silence. "Don't forget, you promised Skye you'd help with her mobility issues. Yoga, remember?"

"I thought that was an unfunny joke."

As I pronounce *joke* with extended, Scottish vowels, an image of Mum flashes up in my mind. *My* mum, Olivia, laughing as I prance around her bedroom doing funny voices. *You should be an actress...*

"The only joke is my wife's body," Rory says, looking me up and down.

I'm wearing thick jeans and a hoodie, hair peeled back in a tight bun, no make-up, as unsexual as I can get. And yet he's still leering.

"Why do you have to say things like that?"

"Because she's an ugly pig. She's revolting. She hasn't gotten me hard in years. A man in my position deserves better."

Last night, after Malcolm started snoring again, I searched for Rory online. He's a marketing executive at a big agency, with a professional photo on his portfolio page, earning at least six figures.

"She admits it herself. You've heard her."

"It doesn't mean I agree."

"You know I could have you on your knees right now, little

Lornie. All day long until Malcolm gets home. Until your jaw dislocates. You should play along. It'll be less work for you."

"Maybe I'll tell Malcolm," I say, staring firmly at the rat. "How would he feel about his brother taking advantage of his wife?"

A flicker of terror crosses Rory's cocky face. There's fear when it comes to his big brother. But he also believes I'm weak. As weak as Lorna.

"He'd be angry. I know that. But he'd be twice as angry if everybody saw those sweet photos of you. If they were online for anybody to take a look at. He'd hate you for not doing everything possible to keep it a secret. And he knows *I* know about Faraday, so let's stop playing games."

Skye walks into the room, looking frankly ridiculous. She's squashed herself into shiny pink workout gear, the leggings skintight, the top squeezing her body.

"Why aren't you dressed?" she snaps, striding right up to me. "Hurry up. What's wrong with you?"

Online, Skye appears in photos at Rory's side, at awards events and social engagements, always looking dignified. From the way Rory looks at her in the photos, anybody would think they were ecstatically married.

I've taken some crap in my time, it's true. But that wasn't really *me*. That was the creature the drugs turned me into. It was easier to swallow pride when my veins were full.

"I'm not in the mood for yoga today."

Skye titters, glancing at Rory; he rolls his eyes as if I'm a disobedient dog.

"In the mood?" she says, glaring at me. "That has nothing to do with it. Your young, tight body is going to teach me how to move. Or will you make me say it? *Faraday*, the magic word, huh?"

"I've already said it, my love," Rory chimes in. "She knows what she has to do."

"Just yoga," I tell her. "Nothing else. I'll be clear upfront. This goes no further."

"Of course not," Skye says with a laugh. "What do you take us for – savages?"

As I get changed, my phone vibrates from the bed. Malcolm.

*Look what I found. See you later x*

And attached, a photo of the notebook.

## 21

---

## LORNA

Eventually, I have to acknowledge what I'm doing.

Sitting with a corpse. The curtains are drawn. The room stinks.

The corpse has had its belly lacerated, and there's blood all over the sofa cushions and the rug, plus spattered all over the sofa itself. I'm going to need to scrub that away. God. There's blood all over my hands, too, and the Stanley knife which lies on its side, the blade looking rusty even though it's new.

How do I get rid of him? I stand, my arms aching, my legs cramped. I've been sitting on the floor, the blood-spattered coffee table between me and the body, not thinking, really, hardly even alive, simply existing near the dead thing.

I'll need cleaning supplies. Bin bags. Something to cut the body with. Or should I take it to the countryside and bury it? For that, I'd need a car.

A knock at my door.

"Hello, Lorna, I'm so sorry. Would I be able to borrow some teabags?"

What the hell does this woman think she's doing?

It's my neighbour, Elizabeth, the one I met yesterday,

gardening in the little courtyard area. She's pushing the door open as if it's the most natural thing imaginable, barging into a complete stranger's home. What's wrong with me? I let the murderous… rage? Pleasure? I let it take me. I haven't locked the fucking door.

"Wait – stop!" I shout, but it's too late.

From the open front door, the older lady looks past the kitchen, through the living room, to the sofa. She can see the corpse. She drops something, maybe her phone, and unfairly, I think, *Good.*

It will make containing this easier. But I don't want to hurt her.

Elizabeth's eyes well up. "Oh, dear Lord, what happened?"

# 22

## SADIE

How does Lorna ever keep a straight face?

Skye is bent over, wheezing with her teeth clenched as her body struggles to maintain the position. Rory stands behind her, his groin pushed against her arse, shifting back and forth and leering at me. He's changed into gym gear, T-shirt and shorts, and I don't think he's wearing underwear.

If they knew how easily spied-on this conservatory was, he might be less enthusiastic. He grinds himself against his wife. "Is that it, Lornie?"

Compared to what I experienced with George and the others – that last time and many before it – this is a joke. It's hard not to smirk at the bastard. "You're doing fine," I say.

Skye bucks as she turns to me, head jostling around. They look freakish, like some bizarre avant-garde theatre performers.

"Is something funny?" Rory stops pumping. "You know where this is going. You know what it's supposed to be like."

Skye straightens, with a visible struggle. "You're not putting any effort in."

Rory approaches. He's got a full-on hard-on as he places his hands on his hips, grinning with that darkness in his eyes.

"Why don't we just get right down to it? On your knees, slut..."

"Oh, yes." Skye giggles from behind him. "This is better."

"Do what you were made for. It's all you're good for. Opening that throat and letting me use it. If you're lucky, my ugly wife might give you some fun too."

"If you're *very* lucky," she says with a strange awe in her voice.

This ugly *thing* happened to me fairly recently. It was the night my baby was conceived. Offers were made; offers were accepted.

But then the rules of the offers stopped mattering, at some point, maybe hour two or three when I was hardly a person at all. Just disembodied meat, a fleshless observer, watching, not feeling, as it, as *I*, was jostled around, hearing horrible wet noises. I was left wondering if I would ever be whole again.

And I will. I am. I say, "No."

Rory laughs, looking at Skye – who grins sickly – and then back at me. "That's not really an option."

"I won't do it." It feels so good to say these words. To treat myself with this kind of respect.

"The thing is, you will though. You've done it before."

"Choked it all down last time we saw each other," Skye says, vile excitement making her seem younger somehow, like her sadism is stripping years from her.

"You like it, when we get down to it," Rory says. He steps forward, reaches out.

I don't think. He has no power over me. Nobody does. Not anymore. Those days are behind me. My hand lashes out, raking down his forearm.

He yells and yanks his hand away, staring as if only seeing me for the first time. He never expected oh-so weak little Lornie to fight back. "Are you mad?" he snaps.

"Faraday," Skye says. "It's the magic word. Have you forgotten the spell, you stupid little whore? You were an eager bitch last time. Doing whatever it took to keep your secret safe."

"You've clearly both got problems," I say, as Rory cradles his arm and Skye looks at him like he should be tearing me to pieces. "Sexual and otherwise. But I want nothing to do with it. Faraday is behind me. Those photos – you can release them if you think it'll make you happy. But all I want is peace for me and my husband." And my baby.

Rory lurches at me, grabbing my arm, wrenching me toward him. Skye titters when he shoves me up against the wall. The air crushes from my lungs. I gasp as he drives his fists against my chest, leaning down. I smooth my hands protectively over my belly.

Skye beams at me. She's never had so much fun.

"We're going to give you a day to remember your manners," he says. "But tomorrow, as soon as Malc leaves for work, you're going to come to *our* room. You'll be ready to behave like the obedient bitch you are. Otherwise, we'll do it. Tell all your neighbours. Tell the world. And everybody…"

"Everybody," Skye whispers.

"Will see you naked, bent over, acting the slut. Think about it tonight. And if tomorrow you decide it's what you want, fine. But you won't. You'll come to your senses."

"Do you think we arranged this trip to see Malcolm?" Skye murmurs. "Don't make us ruin you. Please."

He lets me go, taking a step back.

"I could fucking kill you for that," I yell, raising my hand.

He just grins, eyes narrowed. I've gone too far; I'm not behaving like *little Lornie.* She's scared of Faraday, of the photos. And I should be too. But more than that, I just want to hurt these perverts.

"Tomorrow," Rory says, leaving the room.

Skye lingers. "Don't think of it as a punishment, or anything bad. It's pleasure for us all. It's exciting."

She leaves, and I think about my deadline. Tomorrow... To either do what they want. Degrade myself, again. Or find a way to stop them. My phone vibrates. Another text. Malcolm.

*Tut-tut. Lots of secrets in this journal. You bad girl.*

## 23

---

## LORNA

This is going to win me an Oscar.

I've climbed out of the hole. Maybe it was one of madness or just plain numbness or something else, but now I'm out. I'm *me*. The world has stopped bleeding.

"He tried to force himself on me."

My words come out strangled with sobs. They're not fake, exactly. It's more like I'm letting all the stowed-up sadness of my life pour out, all the things done to me, all the things I've done, aimed at this older woman sitting a few feet from a corpse.

She has her back turned to the dead body, wringing her hands, trembling as she draws in shaky breaths. She's on the verge of collapsing. "Y-you said that," she whispers.

At least she's here. At least she let me lead her to the chair. The small, tatty one that sits on the other side of the coffee table. Miraculously, there's no blood on that one.

"I wasn't sure you heard me. He's done it before, him and others. They all forced themselves on me. I'm pregnant, Elizabeth. And he was *still* going to do it."

This is true, sort of. A half-truth. Jonesy, if given the chance, would have assaulted me without a doubt. Elizabeth looks at me, her eyes red.

"He held the knife to my throat, and he told me I had to do anything he wanted. But I couldn't take it anymore. All I want to do is raise my baby in peace."

"You're pregnant?" Elizabeth asks.

I nod, then bury my face in my hands, erupting into tears. "And I don't even know who the father is. I could've just *killed* the father."

Without looking up, I let the tears continue. My hands are soaked with them. My body shakes just as much as Elizabeth's. This is the most important part, the breakdown. She can't tell anybody.

Finally, she rests her hands on my shoulders. "Oh, dear. It's okay. You didn't mean it."

"I just wanted to make him stop. But he wouldn't. And when he pulled the knife, I panicked. I reacted... and then it was too late." I'm crying into her chest now, as she pulls me into a hug, rubs my back. "I don't know what to do. I'll go to prison."

"It was self-defence," Elizabeth says.

"But I used too much force. I'll go to prison; my life will be over. My *baby's* life will be over before it even begins."

"Oh, Lord. Oh, God. Mary, give me strength. Shine your light on me."

I almost grin, remembering the religious excuse I gave to Sadie in the café. But now's not the time for smiling. It's hard to have any sympathy for Jonesy, though, even if it most definitely wasn't self-defence. It was a feral, unhinged attack.

"Please don't make me go to prison." I weep, gripping Elizabeth's bony shoulders and staring into her eyes. She's a regular person, civilised, and she wants to run; but she also feels my agony, my fear for the unborn child. The conflict wrestles her features. "I won't do that to my baby. If you make me go, I'll get an abor—"

"Don't," Elizabeth cuts in. "Please. For the love of God."

"What other choice do I have?"

Elizabeth finally looks at the corpse, turning very slowly, as if she thinks he's going to wake. "I'll h-help you."

"Help me?"

She swallows. "To get rid of it. But first, you have to promise me you're telling the truth. He tried to... do the unthinkable. And he already has before."

"I swear, it's all true."

I throw my arms around her, then wonder if I've gone too far. But when she returns my hug, I know I've done the right thing. I'm relieved. I may not have to kill this woman.

# 24

## SADIE

I haven't got the luxury of spending the night worrying about tomorrow, about Faraday, about what I'm going to do with Rory and Skye and their threats. I've googled Faraday Cottage, finding an address in Scotland, but nothing else, no hint of what happened there.

The second Malcolm walks into the bedroom, I know this is going to be bad. He stands at the door in his crumpled suit, holding the notebook in his hand, weaving side to side as he walks across the room.

The closer he gets, the more this strange feeling grips me. Mostly, it's disgust; he reeks of booze. But also, it reminds me of the easier days, blackout, no thinking required, no guilt, no doubt, no anything.

"Why would you write all this down?" he says. "What if Rory or Skye had found it?"

It's a good question. I'd never write a journal, listing all my secrets, about Mum and everything else. My *journalism* days, and isn't that a polite word for it. "It hurts, Malcolm, when it's all locked inside."

I've got to go the emotional route. Maybe it was even the truth. God, I'd love to read that book, peel away all her secrets.

"All this stuff about your dad..." Malcolm shakes his head slowly. "I thought we'd agreed, that was behind us. And the way you *whine*. Some people had it far worse than you. Believe me. You, a few scams here and there, and you're playing the goddamned victim. It's pathetic."

My mind struggles to catch everything he's throwing me. Did Lorna's dad make her scam people with him? Did she learn to play a role, like I did, only in a far darker manner, one with far worse consequences? Does that mean she was playing me?

"I'll get rid of it."

"Oh, will you?" He laughs harshly. "I'll just take your word for that, shall I? After your childhood, there's a heading. *My Marriage*. Underlined. You were going to start talking about *us*. Is that what you were going to do last night?"

I shake my head. "I was trying to get the box. That's all I wanted."

"Why so eager, eh?"

I'm not, but it's the only way to maybe escape this punishment. Goddamn, I need to figure out how to make him back off. And Rory. And Skye. Fuck *you*, Lorna.

"And do you just want me to accept," he goes on, his lips watery and his eyes unfocused, "that you just so happened to hide this book in the same place as the box?"

"I'm sorry. I'm stupid. I'm an idiot. I'm too emotional, and it's sad. I need to control myself. Sometimes, I just don't know what's wrong with me. I want to be better, but I—"

"Stop your bloody whining. You've been a bad, bad girl. A real stupid bitch."

"Yes," I whisper.

"Bend over, then. And don't even think about asking for lube."

They're all perverted, all sick in the head. George and Jonesy and Malcolm and Rory, deranged either by life or by something in their blood. Obsessed with inflicting their derangement on others.

What happens next is painful. He does it without thinking of me as a person. I might as well be a sack of flesh without a mind. I only try to make him go a little slower, to inflict the least amount of damage on my body.

But toward the end, he loses control. He's hurting me. I slip away from him, and he tries to follow, so I squirm off the bed and roll away, landing on my back, hands cradling my stomach.

He looms over me, his penis still hard beneath his swollen belly. "What's wrong with you?"

"You have to be gentle."

"There's nothing gentle about you."

"Please."

"Roll over. I'll finish you there."

I sit up. "No."

A fist, and I weave away at the last moment. He catches air and then swipes at me again, like I'm a fly, nothing, insignificant. And maybe I have been, but my child isn't. "I'm pregnant."

His hand pauses; he was about to lunge at me again. "What? How?"

"The pill fails sometimes," I mutter.

I found Lorna's contraceptive medication in the bathroom, so this is a safe gamble, as far as explanations go.

"Jesus. *Christ.*" He stands, his lip curled. "You're not bringing some little brat into this world. You'll have to get rid of it."

I'm tempted to scream, to tell him *no*. But then he turns away, and I don't want to do anything to bring him back. He pulls on his suit and grabs the notebook.

"Did you hear me?" he says, resting his hand on the door.

"Yes," I whisper, my voice raw with all the things I wish I could say instead.

"Disgusting."

A while later, I hear crackling in the garden. I go to the

window to find Malcolm standing at a small bin, the notebook smouldering, all the secrets burning to ash. I hurry to bed, lie down, pretend to sleep. But I won't let myself drift off.

---

Much later, when Malcolm is snoring beside me, I move slowly. So gently, hardly making any noise, holding my breath. I've got to act. To try, at least.

# 25

## · LORNA

"**W**hy are you helping me?" I ask, as Elizabeth drives back toward the city.

She sighs, hands tightening on the wheel, refusing to look at me. Her expression has become hard, but I can tell there's emotion beneath it. It's been a busy night, waiting until it was quiet and then carrying Jonesy down the stairs together, wincing at every noise.

First, we wrapped him: garden bags, then big bags, awkwardly wedged around his body. Finally, we secured it with duct tape. And *then* we hid the whole thing in a thick black rug from Elizabeth's flat. It was awkward, carrying the rug, him – *it?* – and the digging has left my arms sore.

Elizabeth has said little, snapping at me whenever I asked anything. And, ever since we buried the body in the Somerset countryside, in a wild field – an ignored place, hopefully – she's retreated into silence. We washed with water bottles and soap and changed into clean clothes too. We burned the bloodied ones.

I'm attempting to judge her. Is she going to keep this to herself? She's been invaluable so far.

"You can't expect me to believe this is the first time you've ever hidden a body," I say. "You're too good at it."

She glances at me sharply, the landscape black behind her, the sky clear and shining down with bright stars.

"A man did the same thing to me once," Elizabeth whispers, her voice shaking. "I was only sixteen, and he grabbed me... he did what he wanted. My father found out. He was a brutal man, in his way, and he wouldn't let the matter stand."

"He killed him."

Elizabeth nods. "I was the only family he had. My mother died when I was a baby."

"Mine too," I say, wondering if that's the truth. Sadie said our birth mum overdosed. But it's not as if I can trust her.

Elizabeth narrows her eyes, suspicious almost. Maybe she thinks I'm trying to win sympathy, create a connection. "My dad came to me for help. Together, we got rid of that man. I never thought those *skills* would come in useful."

She looks disgusted with herself. "Will anybody come looking for him?"

"I don't think so," I say.

"What about his friends, the ones who..."

"It's okay. You can say it."

She's thinking of what I told her: what George and the others did to Sadie.

"I don't want to." She shudders. "Do they know he's here?"

"Not as far as I'm aware."

"Goodness gracious, girl. You're not filling me with confidence. I suppose all we can do is go on as normal and wait... don't behave suspiciously. I'll keep up with my gardening, and you go on with your... whatever it is you do."

"I'm looking for a job," I tell her.

"Ah, of course. To support your dear child."

I reach over and gently lay my hand on hers. "Thank you so

much. I know you've risked a lot. You could've called the police, but you didn't. You chose to help me. I won't forget that."

"I did it for the baby," Elizabeth whispers, looking at my belly. "I was going to be a mother once, but I had to..." She bites down. "I'm sorry for what he did to you. For what he tried to do. You were right to defend yourself. Let's just hope this is the end of it."

This isn't false gratitude I feel. Without her, I would've been lost. "You're a good person."

She laughs, sounding like she's trying to hold it all together. "He was still a human being. Despite what he did."

"I'd like to spend more time with you. If you'll let me. I don't want to end things this way."

"You can come by for dinner one night," she replies. "But give me some time to process things."

"You're not going to turn me in, are you?"

"If I was going to, I'd tell you first."

"Goodness gracious. You're not exactly filling me with confidence here."

She rolls her eyes at my deadpan delivery, and I even get a smile. I really don't want to hurt her.

---

I sit on the chair, staring at the sofa, the cushions gone. We've scrubbed the sofa itself, and it doesn't *look* or *smell* like blood. It just looks old and tatty. I'll have to replace it soon. Get new cushions, at least. We burned those too, and we scrubbed the floor and every surface until our fingers stung from the chemicals.

The room reeks of them. I almost think I'd prefer blood. It's still dark. This has taken a long time. It's nearly six in the morning, and despite everything, my eyes begin to get heavy.

Then a figure steps from the shadows. I jump to my feet.

# THE PLACES I HURT YOU

You were so innocent. Such a precious and untouched and untouchable thing. Nothing bad would ever happen to you. That was the message in your eyes and your smile and your everything.

You'd always find a way to keep that attractive smile on your attractive face.

There's nothing I can ever say to myself that will justify anything I did. It's as I've mentioned several times: my nature, configuration, the stars inside of me, all of it, it's fire, it's blood, it's melodrama, it's overstatement, it's hunger, it's pain, it makes me ache so deep and so hard I shiver just thinking about it and I hate myself for it.

I'm good, I think. I try to be. Better. But don't blame the Devil for having horns.

Society, in a perfect world, would automatically detect certain tendencies in people and crush their sadist's skulls before they could develop into monsters. The government would hire people to ruthlessly obliterate these types, so that their brains and inner matter spilled out and their skulls split apart, and they'd tell us they were doing right by us, and people like *you* would go along with it because you never learned how to think.

Not *what* to think, but *how*. That's what truly defines a person. Anybody can do something which has been done before. It takes talent to find a unique angle.

The places I hurt you. Fuck. It was wrong, but it was creative. You can't deny that.

# 26

---

## SADIE

"Why so tense?"

Lorna stares at me, seeming annoyed at herself for the panic. I would be too. She looks exhausted, somehow shrunken in her plain T-shirt and blue jeans, her arms skinny as she folds them.

"Did you get another key cut?" she snaps.

"You're too clever for me."

"What do you want? I thought we agreed – we'd deal with our lives alone. You're not supposed to be here."

"And how are you dealing with *my* life?" I ask.

I hope for some response, a flicker of fear to show I made the right choice – to show that Malcolm and Rory and Skye are worth it – but she stares coldly.

"I'm doing well."

"No... unexpected visitors?"

Lorna laughs humourlessly. "You mean one of your many, many, *many* friends? In fact, I've just been to visit *them*. We had a whale of a time. Traded all sorts of stories. Traded lots more, too, if you know what I'm saying."

When my hands smooth over my belly, as if to hide these

words from my baby, Lorna sneers. "You better hope Malcolm doesn't find out about that."

"So you know," I say. "About..."

"George. Jonesy. Who else was there? Benny. Toby. Is that right?"

Their names cut. I force a nod. "If you want answers, you'll need to give me some first."

"Oh, Sadie. You thought I was a complete moron, didn't you?" Despite her words, she seems more relaxed now, dropping into the armchair, folding one leg over the other. The room is filled with the stench of cleaning chemicals, making my eyes sting, and there are no cushions on the sofa. Parts of the sofa are patchy from where the material has been scrubbed. "You thought you'd found a true religious fanatic, somebody who wouldn't even ask a basic question like, *How did Mummy know?*"

I swallow, chest cramping. "I guess I've misjudged a few things."

"You're a very naïve person, I feel."

I take the blow, look for a place to sit. "Did something happen here?"

"I got drunk. Celebrating my freedom. Puked all over the sofa. Oops."

I perch on the arm of the sofa. "Tell me about the box. And what you do with Rory and Skye. What's Faraday – what happened there, at the cottage? If you tell me—"

"You seem to think there's something you can give me," Lorna cuts in. "I've got what I want. A new life. It's what you wanted, too. The difference is, *I'm* making the best of it. I'm handling my – your – problems. You're whining."

"Handling... how?"

"You wouldn't believe me if I told you."

"These are dangerous people."

"I'm sure they are."

"I found your notebook."

Lorna grins. "I made it easy. Same place as the box, right? I thought Malcolm might find it first."

"But why trick me? You're not religious. You didn't believe my reason for wanting to trade lives, did you?"

"You tried to trick *me*. You can't blame me for being angry. That lie you told, about promising your adopted mum... it was ridiculous. So I moved the journal. I told a few lies. Sue me."

"I should do more than sue."

"Look around, *little Lornie*." She grins when her words clearly have an effect. "We're living inside a complete joke."

*Joak*, her Scottish getting strong. It's like some ancient pagan warrior has taken her place.

"You deserve an Oscar as much as I do."

She shrugs. Her eyes have an animal, almost panicked look. It hits me now – she's capable of anything. "Anyway, I tried to warn you. You thought your little rapists were worse than Malcolm and the rest of them? Jesus."

"Who've you talked to?" She studies her fingernails, actually does this. Playing the actress. It's a joke. A *joak*. "Cut the crap, Lor—"

"Nah-uh," she says, switching her accent to English. "Sadie, remember? In fact, you were never Sadie; you've always been Lorna. One day, you'll wake up and realise you imagined this whole thing. You're insane. Reality's bleeding."

With each sentence, she sits up, then stands, then walks over to me. I'm not afraid, exactly, but I don't like when she gets close. "I'm your long lost twin. Let's bond, Sadie. Let's become friends."

"Just, please, tell me. The box. Rory. Faraday. All of it."

"Okay," she says, Scottish again. "Let's seriously think about this. What happens if I don't tell you anything? Is there anything you can do?"

"But... *why*? Everything's falling apart."

She finally looks human again, Lorna from the café, softening. "This wasn't part of the deal. You can't make me talk about this.

It's not fair. You were perfectly willing to let your mongrel friends tear me to pieces. Well, weren't you?"

It's impossible to mask my reaction from her. Goddamn mirror.

"See?" she says. "And now you want my help."

"I could force you to help me. You don't know who I am."

"You don't know who *I* am."

"I've seen things, done things." I get up, walk to her, but I can't get too near. She's got that somehow dangerous look in her pale green eyes. "Don't make me hurt you."

She laughs, and I almost laugh too. At myself. It sounded stupid coming out of my mouth. She's not afraid of me.

"Have you told Malcolm about the baby? No?" Again, she reads me. "Right," she says. "And let me guess. He's told you to get rid of it."

When I nod, she wraps her arms around herself. It's bizarre: a human straitjacket. "We had a baby once, in the beginning. A home birth. A stillbirth. Malcolm threw it against the wall. He was drunk."

"Stop, Lorna."

"He crushed its head, even though it was already dead."

It's too much to hear. Even after everything I've experienced, this is agony. Too ugly to contemplate.

"Lor—"

"After, he threatened the midwife, made her swear she'd never share what happened."

"You're a liar."

There are tears in my eyes. I love my baby so much already. I can't even picture what she described. I won't; I'll think of something else, anything else. I'm supposed to be tougher than this. "How would you explain that?" I wipe away the tears. "There would be… a scene."

"A mess, you mean." She looks at me bleakly. "Believe what you want. But from that day on, he swore he'd never have another child. He said he couldn't deal with the pain. He might not seem like it, but Malcolm is very sensitive, deep down."

"Another lie."

"It's time for you to go. Give me the spare key."

She releases the straitjacket, holding her hand out. This is the moment I say *fuck you*. She can't tell me what to do. But instead, I take the key from my pocket and drop it into her hand. She's acting far too unhinged. Or no, this isn't the act – that was the other her.

"Just give me something. Rory and Skye want to do their weird pervert shit *today*."

"After this, we're done."

"Okay. Yes."

"Tell Malcolm you'll open the box with him, but only if he agrees to let you keep the baby. For Rory and Skye... just do what they want. It never lasts long. Rory is nothing. He's a coward."

"He is?"

"He'll make some threats, but he's nothing like Malcolm."

"But what if I don't want to?" I whisper.

"I know. It's sick. But you've been through far, far worse than those two."

Like last night. My body still aches. The physical agony dragging me back to the dark days with the squeaking mattress and flaking plaster on the ceiling becoming the shape of a butterfly, and then I fly away, on wings of opium.

But last night, it was just me and him. The sickness of it.

"That doesn't mean I want to do it *again*."

"I've given you my advice."

She stares. There's nothing I can do. I leave.

I sneak back into the house, up the stairs. When Malcolm wakes, I tell him. I can't lose this baby. And maybe it will stop him hitting me.

"Are you sure about this?" he says, sitting up in bed, looking ready for brutality. "Because you have to be sure. Or I'll tear that thing out of you and—"

Not again. I can't hear it. "I'm sure."

He leans over, kissing me gently on the cheek, as if he didn't just threaten me, as if last night never happened. What he did to me. The same thing his brother wants to do. "I'll leave it in our special place. Tick tock, Lorna. Time's running out." He laughs almost aggressively, basically coughing in my face. "Do you remember that?"

"Of course." I lay my head against his chest, and he embraces me. "I'll never forget."

# 27

## LORNA

I didn't expect to find Elizabeth gardening so early, not after last night. In the steely overcast light, her features seem more severe.

I stroll over, as friendly as can be. The truth is, I'm still all buzzing nerves after the standoff with Sadie. I was getting more intense than I normally do, but it's not as if anybody could blame me.

His belly was a mess, an ugly painting. Not now – never again. Bury it.

"Hello," I say, when I'm within stabbing distance.

"Hi." She bows her head. "How are you feeling this morning?"

"Shaken up. Terrified. I can't believe I did it." Convincing, and partly true.

"I can imagine. But – well, would you mind not saying hello to me for a while? I don't think we should be seen together. And... I don't want to look at you."

That sounds like guilt and regret. I can't have that. It leads to the desperate need to confess: to be a good person.

"You saved my life. You saved my baby's life."

"I said *enough*," she snaps, shaking all over, like she's going to break down. "Please. I can't."

"Just as long as you..."

"Keep your secret?" I nod, and she sighs in an uncertain way I don't like at all. "I need time to think."

"There's nothing to think about. My baby needs you to stay strong."

"Leave me alone, Sadie. I've asked politely."

She's got a trowel in her hand, the ends flecked with mud. But it could just as easily be stained with liquid red. Stepping forward, I motion to touch her arm. But she steps back, raising the trowel as if she's going to use it as a weapon. Then she drops it to her side, laughing cagily.

"I just want to make sure we're on the same page," I say. "I can't deal with this stress on top of the trauma. It's not good for my baby."

Talk of babies drags me back to that other night, the wicked one. The twisted fairy tale where the prince did the unspeakable. But I did speak it – used it as a weapon against Sadie.

I've never talked about it before.

"Leave me be," Elizabeth says with dignity. "Or I'll be forced to do something I truly do not want to."

Me too, Elizabeth. I hope I'm hiding my anger. "What's that?" I ask.

She reaches into her green overalls, takes out her phone, handing it to me awkwardly in her large gardening gloves. "Go to videos. It's the first one."

She hasn't even got a password. It's an old smartphone, the screen taking a moment to wake up. There's a video folder on the home screen, the other apps scattered about without any organisation.

I click play. "It's your dashcam," I mutter.

I already know what's coming. And there, sure enough, I'm carrying one half of the body, Elizabeth holding the other, both of us walking toward the hole. We're still spattered in dirt, and there's blood all over my clothes, lit by the high beams.

Pressing delete, I hand the phone back to her. I should've buried her in that hole with the rapist.

"I've already made a copy," Elizabeth says, glancing at her phone.

"You're on camera too. This is stupid."

"I'm not saying I'm going to use it. Respect my wishes. I did my part – now let's be strangers."

"With *this* hanging over my head? This is so cruel. You know what he tried to do. What *I* had to do. And now you're adding this stress on top of everything."

She gestures with her trowel. "Dearie, may God bless you, but our conversation is over."

Maybe it is. But *we're* not done. She's just made the worst mistake of her life.

# 28

## SADIE

I stare down at the box. It's metal, black, but chipped so that silver and rust flashes through the façade. The lid is open, showing the handcuffs, the knife, the pills...

The *pills*. They're in a clear plastic tray with marker pen writing on the front. *Morphine*.

The pills rattle around in the tray as I pick it up, and I know this is a problem, how much more interesting they are to me than the other items: the kidnapper's items, the murderer's tools.

My mind goes to bad places, like breaking apart three of the pills and laying the powder in thick white lines on the dresser. If somebody has never tasted that soaring sweet release, they can't understand how tempting it is.

Or maybe if they haven't got memories to bury. Of Jonesy and the others. And before that, the blood, the pain, the crying, the shame. I place the pills down, pushing them across the mattress. Then I pick up the note.

*Find me a perfect girl. No older than twenty. Blonde, beautiful, innocent. Find me a sweet princess, my queen.*

Oh, God. No. This can't be what they do. But if I don't – my baby, the sick story Lorna told. I'm almost crying again just thinking about it.

I nearly yell when there's a heavy knock on the door. "Little *Lorniieeeee*," Rory says, turning the name into a lilting song. "It's time for our morning fun. I thought you might need an escort. Some encouragement. We don't like being kept waiting…"

Grabbing the pills, I shove them in the box then slam it shut. I squeeze the note in my fist, knowing I can't do it, knowing I have to.

Or run. Rob him. That could be a path, but I'd have to figure out how to get access to a *lot* of his cash.

"Lorna." It's Skye, her voice shrill. "This is quite enough."

What's left for me if I leave now – the streets? And with the streets comes everything else. I can't risk poisoning my child with filth. I wonder if a pregnant woman can take morphine.

"*Lorna.*"

Bang, bang, bang, the door trembles in the frame.

"Out. Now. No more games."

"No more games?" Skye says. "I thought that's exactly what we were going to do…"

I turn toward the door, pushing the knife and the pills and the instructions away for now. Distance is what I need, a separation from myself, but without the drugs. But as I walk across the bedroom, I know I can't let this happen to me again.

I'm so tired of being used.

# 29

## LORNA

At the back of the bus, I study the (perfectly legal and easily purchasable) lockpicking kit in my lap. It's one of the skills my kind, doting, loving father taught me.

What a man. What a hero he was.

Elizabeth lives in flat number twenty-one. I remember that fact as I walk toward our building. She's still in the garden, on her knees, wheezing as she tugs at weeds. She goes at it obsessively, as if blotting out what we did.

She looks up, sees it's me, then immediately goes back to her work. Good. Let her obsess.

I'm finding that video: a hard drive, memory stick, laptop. I just hope she hasn't uploaded it to the Cloud. But there could be something else too, maybe a keepsake of hers, something with emotional value.

She's not the only one who can play the blackmailing game.

In my flat, I put on a face mask and pull my hood up, and then put on some surgeon-style gloves. I'm not going to commit a crime – well, a serious one, one that would bring forensics – but better safe than sorry.

Up the stairs, I move quickly, rushing to her door. I kneel and handle the lockpick tools with practice. The *click* doesn't take long; it never does, not with how many times I've done it, tinkering with locks as a girl, Dad smiling proudly, and me stupid enough to value it.

When I push the door open, a little girl stares at me.

She's a toddler, wearing a pink one-piece, a teddy bear dangling from its leg between her fingers. She opens her mouth. I raise my finger to *shh* her, but it's too late. She screams.

From deeper in the flat, footsteps pound toward me.

## 30

## SADIE

We're back to the weird yoga routine, in the living room this time, the curtains drawn, the doors closed. I thought they were going to take me to the bedroom. But something about yoga and being in communal areas seems to turn the freaks on. Skye shifts against Rory; he's ogling me as he thrusts back and forth, his hands on her hips. He even runs his tongue over his lips, the freak.

"Careful," Skye says, bucking her hips. "You'll crack my old bones."

They're not even pretending to be here to workout this time, no exercise gear. Skye wears a billowing dress that shows her pale, bony knees. Rory is wearing a vest and shorts, his *thing* outlined clearly.

I'd love to cut it off. The note tries to invade the moment. The mission. But I can't think about that yet. Lorna, what have you done? What have you let your *husband* do?

"Such a weak slut," Rory says.

We've been at this for at least ten minutes, maybe more. Rory gives Skye a shove. She collapses forward, falling onto the sofa, and then Rory spins on me. His lips are wet from where he's been licking them. He couldn't look grosser if he tried.

He's a coward; I remind myself of that, as he swaggers across the room, not ashamed by his hardness at all.

Lorna would do what he says. Follow whatever sick orders he gave her, just like she did with Malcolm, presumably: the box, the girl, *no older than twenty.*

He didn't give a *minimum* age. Rory backs me up to the door, then I stop, not wanting to be pressed against it. I may need to run.

Behind him, Skye rises to her feet, lurking in the background like a vulture ready to feast. She doesn't seem bothered about the fact her husband just assaulted her.

Maybe he does it often. I don't care. I can't pity her.

"Okay, Lornie." Rory strokes his hand up and down the front of his shorts. "No more messing around. I've got you. I *own* you. There's nowhere for you to run."

He steps closer. Soon, he'll have me wedged up against the door. My baby, my sweet baby... I'll be a good mother. And that means being a good person. Strong, capable of defending myself and my child.

He's leaning in as though for a kiss. Before, I could've taken it, endured his watery lips pushed against mine. I would've hated every second, but only on one level, the core of *me*; the rest of my mind would be somewhere else, morphine land, just a pill, crack it open, a line, just a line—

No. *Fuck* no.

Rory yells when I rake my fingernails down his face.

# 31

## LORNA

I rush down the corridor, quickly pulling off the mask, pulling my hood down. The footsteps are getting too close; they'll be able to see me soon, whoever they are.

I closed the door after I darted away from the little girl; it's opening now, whining on the hinges, ancient and half-broken like everything in this place.

Stuffing the mask into my pocket, I turn, walking back up the way I just came. I do it casually, as though I didn't hear the girl scream: as though I didn't *cause* it.

A man steps from the house, the child in his arms. He's around my age, if I had to guess, with a haircut I should find absurd: the sides shaved, a thick braid on top, some sort of wannabe Viking. But his eyes draw me in, somehow, like Malcolm's did once.

Nope – no attraction. I can't even contemplate that. I should be too ruined after all Malcolm has done to me. And Dad. And Rory. And Skye.

"Is something wrong?" I say, all innocence as he strides toward me.

"Uh…" He pauses, handsome and fit in his gym T-shirt and

shorts, tribal tattoos snaking up his arm. "Did you see anybody just now?"

I look over my shoulder, which is maybe a tad too much, like this mystery person is going to miraculously appear.

"No, why, is something wrong?"

Who *are* these people? Either they live with Elizabeth, or – more likely – she lied to me when she gave her flat number as twenty-one. Or I'm remembering it incorrectly. But I'm sure I'm not. Unless reality is bleeding more than I thought.

"What's wrong, bug?" the man says, rocking his child.

The girl turns in his embrace, looking at me with wide innocent eyes. The love this man has for his daughter is enough to make me respect him. Somehow, I know he'd never hurt her, or force her to do things, become somebody she never wanted to be.

"You're pretty," she says, and the man laughs.

"A lot of fuss for nothing, then." He rolls his eyes at me with a grin. "I thought... well, it doesn't matter. I'm Finn, by the way. I take it you live in the building?"

I nod. "Yes. I'm L... Sadie."

There's something about Finn that makes it difficult to stubbornly continue my role. He's got this cheeky look, his daughter wearing the same expression, as though both of them are troublemakers.

"Is something wrong?" I ask.

He's glancing up and down the hallway.

"Is it Momma?" the girl says, her voice lilting, babbling, and something in me starts to melt.

It's the piece of me which should've frozen for good the night of the horror. But there's no denying it; she's adorable, especially the little green bow in her hair, her teddy still hanging from her hand.

"No," Finn says tightly. "Nice to meet you, Sadie."

"And you," I reply. "If you ever need anything..."

Why am I making this offer? I killed a man not even a full day ago.

"You only have to ask." I smile at him, then at the girl. "Before you go, what's *your* name, huh?"

"Buggy bug," she says, laughing. "The, the, the *queen* of bugs."

"Her name's June," Finn says, turning away.

*What happened to her mother?* I almost ask, thinking of June's question, the tightness in Finn's expression. But this is none of my business. I'm long past wilfully throwing myself into somebody else's mess.

Marching downstairs, I go outside to the courtyard. Elizabeth is going to give me some answers, starting with: why lie about her flat number? That was *before* she helped me hide the body.

But she's not here anymore. Then – it's weird – it's like I *feel* her staring at me.

She's standing at the top window, so her flat must be in the thirties. I'm not quite sure about her expression – maybe it's the light and the distance and the angle distorting things – but I think she's smirking.

# A TRULY INSANE INDIVIDUAL

Nobody believes you, has ever believed you. That's what you've never understood. It's all about perception, about reading the mind of the person who's observing, judging what they need to see, then becoming that. That way, you can ensure the other person – you – seems ridiculous.

It's an old trick. It's a good one. It actually makes me sick, how easily people will accept what somebody shows them. It can be the simplest ruse sometimes, the most subtle deception, and, wide-eyed and naïve, people will accept it.

Even people like you, those who believe they are smart, if orchestrated in the right way, will crumble and become pliable. I know you don't like it when I speak like this, but I think we both know it's the truth.

We both *should* know, anyway, but maybe you're playing games. Maybe you're pretending you're suddenly and inexplicably better than that.

Smarter, more capable, when that's laughable. You're nothing. You'll always be nothing. That's how I know I'm not a psychopath. I can read people, understand them. A truly insane individual would not be able to do that.

# 32

## SADIE

I've managed to run upstairs and lock myself in the bathroom. Rory hammers his fist against the door. This isn't a new occurrence for me: cowering on one side of the door as a man huffs and puffs on the other. Some people take drugs and become sedated, barely conscious drawlers, and others remember every bad thing that's ever happened to them and decide to take it out on the world.

Was Lorna lying when she said he's not dangerous? It's not as if I can trust her. Rory stops hammering, sighs loudly.

"This is really getting out of hand," Skye says, her voice soft.

"I fucking know. What else am I supposed to do?"

"It was never like this before."

"Lorna," Rory snaps. "Open the door now."

"You don't want me to do that."

"Oh, really?"

"If you make me open this door, I'm going to hurt you. Maybe not right away. Maybe you'll be able to…" I can't say it, can barely even look at it in my thoughts. "Do what you want. But you'll have to kill me. Otherwise, I'll find a way to end you both."

Now *I* slam against the door, not having to fake the anger.

The bravery, I'm faking some of that, fine, but not the rage swelling in me.

Now I'm pounding my fists, remembering last night, the agony of what Malcolm did, and the note – the evil note. *Find me a perfect girl.* I hit the door harder, my knuckles aching, cutting, bleeding, and my voice is raised; I hardly even hear what I'm saying, disconnecting like I did in my *journalism* days.

"I'll kill you both. I've done it before."

This isn't true. But a shade of it is.

"I'll treat you like meat. I'll—"

I abruptly stop, realising I've let my accent lapse back into English.

"Don't be stupid," Rory says.

"Did you hear her accent?" Skye asks a moment later.

"What about it? Lorna – get out here. I swear to God…"

"Her voice. It changed. Didn't you hear it?"

"You're a mad, stupid bitch. Marrying you was the worst thing I ever did. Shut up."

"I heard it."

I freeze, listening to their voices, guessing where they're standing based on that. This can't go on, and it's not as if the agony has gone anywhere. My mind is red with memories from the journalism and all the reasons for my escape.

I go to the mirror cabinet and take out Malcolm's shaving set. There's a straight razor in here.

"Do you want us to take you to the bunker?" Rory snaps, and Skye makes one of her tittering noises as if the idea is the most exciting thing she's ever heard.

*Bunker?*

"It used to be some boring survivalist prison," Skye says, giggling. "But we've made some improvements. Lots of fun things for you to do there, little Lornie. But you might not like it."

I take slow breaths, wondering if they're being serious. If they have some kind of underground shelter in their home, going there is the last thing I'd ever want. "And no neighbours to hear you scream," Skye goes on.

"If you do what you know you should, we'll even treat you like a human being in the bunker. Most of the time, anyway. You remember the deal, don't you? You remember what we said? But you have to make *sure* it's done."

"If she survives…" Skye trails off.

I say nothing – I've got no clue what or who they're talking about – as I stare down at the straight razor, wondering if I've got the guts to really do this.

Rory bangs on the door again. "Get your ass out here. I've got an appointment with it." Holding the blade to the light, I study the sharp edge. This has to be done.

Standing at the door, I clasp the small metal lock between my thumb and forefinger, getting ready to turn it.

They'll be sorry. This is what *has* to happen. Focusing on my accent, I say, "You know messing with me or my husband is a bad, bad idea. I'm giving you one last chance. Back. Off."

A long moment. I think maybe he'll see sense.

But then he punches the door again. "Enough! Out! Now!"

I don't let myself flinch, waiting as he starts hitting it again, over and over. Like a beat, like music, I listen, timing him, and then I turn the lock and quickly grab the handle, wrench the door open.

He spills in, the momentum carrying him past me.

I leap forward, grab Skye's hair. She doesn't even try to defend herself, instead looking past me, at Rory, as if he's going to rescue her. By the time she realises she's in trouble and starts squealing, I've already got a big bunch of hair in my hand.

Twisting it, I force her to her knees. I'm panting. My chest hurts. My belly throbs, as if my baby doesn't like this.

"Stop!" I scream, bringing the razor to Skye's throat.

Rory glares, fists clenched. "Cut the bitch. Do you think I care?"

I don't want to do this, but I have to be strong. I have to be more than an observer this time.

Skye moans as I push the blade against her skin. I can't see her throat from this angle, but I can see Rory's eyes, the path they make as they follow something from the razor down her skin. It must be blood.

I push harder, and she tries to move away from the blade. It's simple to keep her in place with her hair.

"I'll kill you both," I say. "You're nothing to me. This has gone on long enough. If you want to spread the photos of me, do it. If you want to spread rumours about Faraday, go ahead… But this is *done*. And don't think me or Malcolm will take it lying down."

Rory almost continues playing the tough guy. He straightens his back, gets ready. But when I mention his brother, the same fear from dinner floods his features. He becomes a scared little boy.

"You won't tell him," Rory says. "That would mean admitting to what we've done."

"Yes, you both blackmailed and assaulted me. Maybe he'll blame me. Maybe he'll hurt me. Fine. I'm used to it. But he'll blame you *more*."

I push the blade even harder against Skye's skin, and suddenly, Rory remembers he's supposed to care about his wife. "You're hurting her."

"Are we done?"

"Let her go."

"Are we *done*?"

"Yes!" he yells. "All right? Your pussy's not that special."

I throw Skye at his feet. This is the most dangerous part, where he could charge at me. But he doesn't. Instead, he kneels, holding Skye. The cuts on his face – from where I scratched him – weep a drop of blood.

"If you try and touch me again…"

Rory won't look at me. "Like I said, you're not that bloody special."

———

I hide in the bedroom for the rest of the day, the door locked, attempting to ignore the box in the corner. And what's inside.

It's boring and stressful, lying here as Skye and Rory bang around in the spare room. I'm not sure what they're doing until Malcolm rings.

"Rory said he's leaving early."

I bite down, waiting for him to go on: to tell me Rory has revealed the truth. He's told him about the photos.

"Oh?" I say, when Malcolm doesn't say anything else.

"So don't cook anything extravagant tonight. It'll be just the two of us. Plenty of time to talk…"

"Did Rory say why they're going?"

"A work thing. Who cares? I was getting sick of him anyway. It's time for life to finally start being interesting again."

# 33

## LORNA

I know which flat Elizabeth is staying in now... assuming I *did* see her in the window, that reality wasn't bleeding again. It was a simple case of going to the correct floor and aligning myself with the courtyard below.

Looking up and down the hallway, I get ready for the chance that I'm about to walk in on somebody. But it's got to be now. Elizabeth just left holding several bags-for-life wrapped around her fist like a makeshift boxing glove. I work quickly, thanks *Dad*, the lock clicks and I push the door open.

Right away, I know it's her flat. It has a light and airy feel, with framed landscape paintings on the wall, nothing specific to her, but somehow warm. A well-tended plant sits in a pot in the corner, leaves clawing out like fingers from a grave. Or maybe that's me being morbid.

I pass the kitchen to my left – spotless – and then the living room, like mine but far cleaner, with more plants. Magazines are piled on a wooden, chic coffee table. Most of the magazines are gardening, but there's a style one there.

*Don't let your age steal your shine!*

Even if I'm doing this, *have* to do it, I feel a pang of regret.

Elizabeth is a beautiful woman and doesn't need these magazines. The bathroom is as spotless as everywhere else. There are few personal items scattered around, no photos. In the bedroom, it's different. There are photos.

Lots of them, stuck to a large noticeboard which itself hangs from the wall, the colourful pins jutting out of the upper parts of the printer paper.

I walk over the plush, earth-coloured rug. The bed is well-made, the sheets tucked in, with an ornate bedside cabinet. It has a golden handle and a large keyhole on the front.

The photos are so bizarre. It's the man from earlier, the one whose daughter I scared, with the Viking braid and the handsome – no, *not* handsome, I don't care – smile. There are photos of him holding his daughter, June… or *buggy bug*, as she called herself.

I grin thinking of that, lips twitching beneath my mask. His name was Finn, I remember.

Photos of him standing at the window. In coveralls outside what looks like a warehouse. Climbing into a car. Sitting in a café reading a newspaper. Picking June up from some sort of playgroup, bright letters in the background.

This is the sort of thing *I* used to do. Before my escape. Is that it? Is Elizabeth like – not me, Malcolm? Is she like my ex-husband?

That's how I've come to think of him. I can't think of us as married anymore. I've become too lost in thought. Footsteps behind me.

I turn – too late.

It's Elizabeth, with no shopping, eyeing me with a predator's calm.

## 34

### SADIE

Malcolm touches my battered hand as though he didn't assault me last night. He cradles it almost gently, as we stand in the hallway, and I wonder if this is why Lorna agreed to the box. This kindness; the transition from hell to something approaching life.

"What happened?"

I've thought about this. I can use it to my advantage.

"Rory kept mentioning Faraday. I lost my temper. It's not fair. I almost hit him, but he moved, and…"

"You hit the wall?" he says.

I nod, wincing as he casually smooths his thumb over the cuts, a result of slamming my fist against the door when hiding in the bathroom.

"That's why he left," Malcolm says in disgust, striding past me. "He's got some nerve, talking about Faraday."

I follow Malcolm into the living room, hungry for scraps. "I couldn't believe it either."

We sit together on the sofa. My hands naturally spread across my belly, a protection in case he turns into a monster again.

"It's typical Rory, using that to try and make himself feel important. Pathetic. What did you tell him?"

"That I never wanted to speak about Faraday. It belongs in the past."

Malcolm looks at me sternly. This answer matters.

"It's too painful," I say, bowing my head.

He sighs darkly. "I understand. That one got out of hand. I never should've done anything on a family holiday. I know, I know… I was wrong. You don't have to tell me."

"I didn't say that."

"But you're *thinking* it. Jesus, Lorna, relax. I'm not angry at you. I agree. But if she was supposed to be Rory's girl, why was she making eyes at me all damn night? And why did she let me *kiss* her, eh? And then, oh no, she had to turn cold. Pretend like she didn't want it."

My stomach cramps. Is there anybody good in this whole sick tale?

"It's not fair, is it?" Malcolm demands.

"No," I say, the only answer I can give.

"It's not like *you* did anything, anyway. Well – you helped, but that was it."

Helped how?

Malcolm smirks, reaching over to me. It takes every shred of self-control not to flinch away from him. When he places his hand atop mine – pushing so that my hand is firm against my belly – I almost scream.

"You can be so fierce. I thought she might go around telling stories after it was all done. But after you put the fear of God in her, I knew we weren't going to have any problems."

So let me get this straight, Lorna. Your husband assaulted his brother's girlfriend and then *you* scared the woman into shutting up.

"You're going to need that part of yourself again now," he goes on. "I haven't felt a single thing since moving here. I've been dead.

Sleepwalking through life, through a shitty job, through everything. But with the box open, it's like... ah..."

He grins, letting out a long breath, a hungry man finally sitting for a meal.

"It's like I can finally let myself feel something. A flicker of hope, of fun. Of humanity. Don't call me a hippy. I know that's how I sound."

There's a joking tone in his voice, so I do what's expected of me. I smile and laugh, while inside I'm scrambling for ways to end this. Rob him, run?

When I searched the house, I found no evidence of bills or financial records, no deed to the house, nothing. Perhaps he keeps these elsewhere, in a safety-deposit box or some other safe place. A regular woman would run, no matter what.

"When are you going to start your search?" Malcolm says, pushing my hand aside, lifting my shirt, laying his cold, clammy palm right against my belly.

If my baby could kick, it would break every one of Malcolm's fingers to get him away. He pushes against me. I'm taking too long.

"Soon," I murmur.

"Soon? That's not very specific."

"Tomorrow."

He withdraws his hand. "Good. Visit me at work. I might be able to help."

"Why?"

"I've got somebody in mind. A good place to start, anyway. You should be happy. You've got one hell of a supportive husband. I'm doing half the work for you."

"What do you want me to do?"

"The usual."

*What's the usual?* "Okay, Malcolm. I'll come to your office tomorrow." Where *is* his office? "Actually," I quickly add, "do you think I can get a lift with you? I could do some shopping in the morning."

"For what? You've got everything you need here."

"I'd like to look at the baby stuff. Then I can meet you at lunchtime?"

"I wish I could let myself be excited about this," he says, snatching his hand away. "But fine – we'll do it your way. As long as you pull your weight…"

"I will."

"Because if you don't," he says, ignoring me. He gestures to my stomach. He doesn't have to finish.

# 35

## LORNA

"**A**re you going to tell him?"

Elizabeth sits hunched in the chair, tapping her fingernail against her cup of tea. When she first walked in, I thought she was going to turn feral. There was this look in her eyes, as if she was ready for violence.

But now, I wonder if I was projecting. She broke down, her voice straining as she demanded to know why I was there.

*"You threatened me. I'm sorry, but I had to fight back..."*

Any sane woman wouldn't have accepted this as an excuse for breaking into somebody's home. But Elizabeth clearly isn't sane, or anything close to it. She helped a stranger hide a body, and now she's stalking Finn and his daughter.

"Lorna?" she snaps, sitting up.

"So you're saying he's your son."

She winces. "I'm not just *saying* that. He is. I had to give him away when I was younger. Life was... well, that's the way of youth. You think life is far harder than it is. Then you get older and look back, and realise there's so much you could've done."

"You tracked him down."

"Yes. I'm not ashamed of it. I paid a large fee to a private detective so I could find my boy and…" She pauses, clenching her jaw. "My sweet granddaughter."

"Why don't you just introduce yourself, then?" I say. "Why take all those photos, and hang them up like a serial killer?"

"A *serial killer*? Jesus, give me strength. I'd never hurt a soul. And definitely not them."

"Why did you give him away?"

The parallel to my own life makes me suspicious, wary in a way I can't quite identify. She's got long-lost family just like I have. She's reconnecting in a bizarre and grisly fashion just like me.

"I'm scared," she whispers. "He might want nothing to do with me. At least, this way, I can get to know him on some level."

I try not to show my reaction. Distrust, my mind thrumming as I try to work out what's really going on here. Or maybe this is it, a sad, lonely woman clinging onto a life she never had to begin with. "Why did you come home so soon?"

"What?"

"You left the building clearly on your way to go shopping. You came home minutes later without any shopping. Why, Elizabeth?"

"I…"

"Because," I go on, when she trails off, "some people might think you planned it on purpose. You left, perhaps knowing I wanted to do some investigating… and then you came back at the exact right time."

"Lord, no." She looks at me like I'm mental. "I forgot my Clubcard, that's all."

"And before, when you gave Finn's flat as yours? That was before the…" The murder. "You helped me," I finish. "You had no reason to lie. But you did."

"I don't understand," she says.

"When we met, you told me you lived in flat twenty-one."

"I did?" She's playing with me.

"You made a point to mention it."

"I was being friendly. If I told you I lived in twenty-one, it's because Finn was on my mind, that's all. I didn't lie. Anyway, I think breaking and entering is *far* worse than a simple lapse in memory."

"What about stalking?"

She narrows her eyes. The predator is back for a moment. Or am I imagining it? "What about murder?" she snaps.

I bow my head, summon tears. When they don't come, I make a sniffling noise. "You know why I had to do that. All I want is to go on with my life. All I want is for my baby to be safe and loved... without the prospect of prison hanging over my head."

"The dashcam video."

"What else?"

"So you were here to find something with which to blackmail me – even after I told you I needed time?"

There's no tactical advantage to lying. "Yes."

Elizabeth sighs, finally taking a sip of her tea. It was the most British thing imaginable, when she offered her intruder – me – a cup. I declined, but it didn't stop her boiling the kettle.

"What if we made a deal?" she asks. I wait, and she goes on. "It's tiring work, watching over my son. What if you helped?"

This is exactly what I've been trying to escape. But Elizabeth presumably doesn't want to kill her long-lost child. "How?"

"Get to know him. Ingratiate yourself. There's only so much I can learn by watching."

I grit my teeth. My body is sore and tired from last night, my mind no better. But I can't imagine splitting this woman's skull or slitting her throat. It won't fit into my mind for some reason.

"You're being very vague," I say. "How long do I have to do this for?"

"A week," she replies. "I think that's fair, considering everything I've done for you."

"Fine." It will give me some time, at least. "But after that, no more games."

"Oh, this is *excellent*. When will you start?"

She's suddenly become a mother hen, intent on matchmaking.

"Tomorrow. I need sleep."

And, hopefully, not dream. Nothing, a bottomless pit of soundless emptiness, that's all I want.

## 36

## SADIE

"I'll see you at lunch," Malcolm says, pushing the car door open.

He works in an office on the Bristol waterfront, a tall, red-brick building with a bright graphic above the door. I leave the car, inhaling the cool morning air.

At least I know where he works now, but I'm not sure walking around Bristol, shopping, is a good idea. What if somebody recognises me, one of the dealers I met the night I almost lost my resolve?

I turn, meaning to walk away, but Malcolm clears his throat. Like an obedient pet – hating myself – I return to him. He pulls me into an embrace, kissing the top of my head.

"We're in public, remember," he whispers. "At least pretend to love me."

"I *do* love you."

"Good girl."

He walks toward the office, but then he stops, suddenly turns back. His smile becomes more and more difficult to believe as he approaches. Finally, it's more like he's baring his teeth. "And don't forget, just because I've put in work with Rachael, you still have to hold up *your* end. I've only got so much patience."

He leaves, and I walk the other way, along the waterfront, heading from the centre. I'll walk the outskirts of Bristol, find a quiet café, and then return when it's time to…

I swallow. Time to *meet her.* The woman we're going to do unspeakable things to.

I force a smile, repress a shiver, remembering the note. *Find me a perfect girl. No older than twenty. Blonde, beautiful, innocent. Find me a sweet princess, my queen.* "I know."

---

When I return to the office – my sore legs and lower back giving me a preview of what *real* pregnancy will be like; I'm weirdly looking forward to it – Malcolm is leaning against his car, talking to somebody.

She's a young woman, looking more like a teenager, with blonde hair tied up in a bun. Her cheeks are incredibly red, almost comic-book-like. She's got wide naïve eyes and an expression which annoys me; it's too innocent.

Malcolm turns; she looks at me, and her face says, *I'm so mature, so world-wise, nothing can ever hurt me.* It's what I was like, once. Before Mum, before the *journalism,* before the drugs.

"Lorna." Malcolm's public mask is effective, his warm tone convincing. "This is Rachael, the woman I was telling you about. A real up-and-comer in the company. A long overdue meeting, and *that's* an understatement."

Rachael stupidly beams. "You're too kind."

It's oh-so civilised as she offers me her hand. Malcolm beams behind her, the proudest little prick in class, as if he's showing off a project. He's got such a sick look in his eyes, so excited, so ready for…

"It's nice to meet you," she says, eyeing me stiffly. *Why isn't your wife taking my hand, Malcolm?* I imagine her thinking. Quickly, I offer mine, and we shake. "I've heard so much about you."

About Lorna, she means. She's probably knows more than me.

"Are you sure you don't mind watching my little one?" Oh, Jesus. No. Don't let that be true. She looks too young to have a child. "My mum usually takes him but she's busy."

She'd just let a complete stranger watch over her child. Malcolm steps forward. "She's already told me it's completely fine, Rachael. You have to think about your career too."

"He's taking me to a financial seminar. I've never been to one before. I don't think they'll let me through the door."

"You've got talent," Malcolm says. "It would be their fault if they didn't see it."

"As long as it's okay?" She's eyeing me again, this absolute moron, this fucking idiot.

"How old is your…"

*Son? Daughter?* She said her mum usually takes *him*. My mind is so slow sometimes.

"Son?"

Malcolm laughs roughly. "I've already told you. A cute little sixteen-month-old boy. Just don't get too attached. You might give me ideas."

Rachael giggles. "You'd make great parents."

"I guess you should see this as a test run then, Lorna."

Both of them, all teeth: one mouth split open in a predator's bite and the other is a mouth waiting for a gun. Like she's already sucking on the barrel.

"Right." Malcolm claps his hands. "Let's drop Lorna off, and then we'll get to the seminar. How does that sound?"

"Uh, pretty much amazing!"

Malcolm opens the back door and waves her inside, then walks to the driver's door, staring at me. He lowers his voice to an aggressive whisper. "You already know how old her little brat is. Why are you acting stupid?"

So Malcolm's talked about her before. I've got to stop putting myself out there like that.

"How long do I have to watch him?" I ask.

"The seminar won't last more than a couple of hours. Anyway, this is good. Make friends. Be nice."

"Are you really taking her to a seminar?"

He grins, shrugs, then opens the car door. "Are you excited?" he says, looking in the rear-view as though speaking to a child.

## 37

### LORNA

There's a police car parked outside the building.

I peel the curtains apart, staring as two officers climb out. One is a tall, wide-shouldered man, red hair just about visible beneath his hat. The other is a lean woman with a tight yellow ponytail, her hand resting on her hip. They laugh as they walk through the courtyard, exchanging some pig banter.

That's not fair. That's Dad coming out in me. I was always taught to hate the *rashers*; that was Dad's term. He would often say he could smell them from miles away. Not that it helped him.

Who rang them? Who cares about Jonesy enough... and knows he came *here*?

Maybe he told the others. I'm still wondering about Sadie's *friend*, the one who tracked me down. I should've asked her when she sprung out on me, but the killing was too fresh in my mind. Or maybe somebody saw us moving the body. But there's no knock at the door. No pounding footsteps.

About fifteen minutes later, the police officers re-emerge. The man shrugs and the woman says something that makes the man laugh. They leave, and then Finn comes walking out, wearing a white vest that shows his tattoos. He's immediately identifiable by his braid. He's smoking, trembling with each motion of the cigarette to his lips.

This is the perfect opportunity to go and speak with him. To do what Elizabeth is *telling* me. That old bitch. Bossing me around. It doesn't help that I sort of like her. Was she the one talking to the police?

---

"Hard day?" I ask, shouldering Sadie's punky pin-covered bag. I'm pretending to be leaving the flat.

Finn turns, grunts, nods. Far less friendly than last time.

"Did you see those police just now?"

He tosses his cigarette butt. "It would be hard not to. They were standing at my bloody door."

I didn't expect *this*. Elizabeth, or something drug-related with one of the other residents. The hallways reek of weed. It's a disgusting smell.

"Oh," I mutter.

"I'm sorry. This is none of your business."

"Sometimes, people need to vent."

"Yeah, but I've already tried that."

"Can I have one of those?" I ask, when he takes out a pack of cigarettes.

Malcolm hates smoking. So do I, really, but it's a convenient way to keep the conversation going. I can't want this man, find him attractive, or even interesting.

Once Elizabeth has deleted that video, she's out of my life; including her son, her grandchild, if that's what they really are. When he hands me the lighter, our hands touch.

We smoke quietly for a minute. My head swims. My mouth tastes like ash.

"My bloody ex-missus," he says, sighing. "She's been spreading crap about me on Facebook. Saying I mistreat June. She *knows* she's not allowed to spread stuff. It was in the court order, for *fuck's* sake." He grits his teeth, then glances at me as though only just remembering I'm here. "I'm sorry."

"You don't have to keep apologising. It sounds like you have every right to be angry."

"Never marry a sociopath, that's all I'll say." Oops. "But I really am oversharing now," he goes on.

"I honestly don't mind."

"And I promised June I'd quit these things."

"She knows about cigarettes, at her age?"

He sighs. "She knows about lots of things she shouldn't."

"I suppose I'm surprised she has an *opinion* on them, then."

"She's very opinionated," he replies, smile not faltering, his love for his daughter so clear I immediately side with him over the mother, which is stupid. He could easily be lying.

"Where is she now?"

"With my dad. I was supposed to be working this morning. But I show up – and they haven't got anything for me. Lucky, I guess. At least I was here to talk to my best bloody pals."

"Where do you work?" I ask.

"On the bins." He lowers his eyes, as if he should be ashamed. "When I can get the days."

"I don't even have a job," I tell him. "So stop bragging, all right? You're making me jealous."

He chuckles. "Yeah, I know, I can't stop telling people."

"Is June safe?"

"I spoke to my dad. I'm going to get her now." He pauses, tilts his head, laughs as though at himself. "This is going to sound crazy, but do you want to come, Sadie? She really liked you."

No – I don't. I can't give a single *shit*. But Elizabeth's given me no choice.

"That sounds lovely."

# 38

## SADIE

"Bang, boom, bang."

The horrible part of this is that Riley is a cute little boy. He's sat in front of a small magnetic panel, picking up dinosaur shapes and tossing them at it. They stick with a *clunk*, or sometimes bounce off. Either way, he laughs, lost in his own world.

Rachael and Riley live on an estate somewhere between rough and okay. The gardens are overgrown or filled with objects – washing machines, old bikes, bricks – but I didn't spot any bad vibes when Malcolm dropped me off. And my senses are tuned for that sort of thing.

"Mama, bad," he says.

I'm not really listening, more staring at the gameshow on the TV, thinking about what Malcolm and Rachael are doing. Maybe it is a seminar of some kind. Maybe it's sex.

I wouldn't care about that, obviously. Let him screw who he wants. But if it's something box related... He brutally assaulted somebody in Faraday, his brother's *girlfriend*.

"Mama, bad, bad, bad."

The magnetic panel falls over when Riley shoves it.

"Hey." I kneel, standing it up again. "You don't like your toy?"

"Bad, bad, bad." He falls back, kicking his legs and waving his arms. *"Bad, bad, bad! Bad, bad, bad!"*

"Riley, stop it." He ignores me, screaming the word over and over again. The walls are thin in here, the faded wallpaper almost seeming to shake with each yell. "Riley."

But he won't listen. Here I am, thinking about motherhood twenty-four-seven, and I can't even calm him down. In the end, I stop trying, returning to my chair and folding my arms. I stare stubbornly at the TV.

Let the neighbours complain. It's not my problem. God, what I'd give for a— No, not that. Never that. I move my hand over my belly.

Riley stops after a minute or two, rolling over and clambering to a kneeling position. He looks annoyed that I didn't take the bait. Now, he shows his gap teeth, grinning, tantrum forgotten.

"Mama *bad*," he says good-naturedly.

"I'm sure she is," I reply, not letting myself care.

"Bad, bad, *bad*."

"Fine, Riley. Would you care to explain all the ways in which your mother is a bad person? I'd be very interested to hear your insight and opinion on the topic."

His mouth drops open, and then he falls to his side. *"Bad-bed-bad-bed."*

It's difficult to pick through the babbling rhythm of his words, but I'm sure he said *bed*.

*"Don't tell don't tell don't tell."*

"Riley." My sharp voice snaps his head around. I lean forward, mind spinning. "Are you saying *bed* or *bad*?"

He smiles widely. I swear, he's cleverer than he's letting on. It's like there's a schemer somewhere behind his innocent face. Or is that just madness? Does he even know what he's saying? It's striking me I know very little about children.

He goes on with his song, *bad-bed-bad-bed*. Maybe this is the junkie in me, but I can't resist having a look. I've done similar things countless times, rooting through people's belongings.

I'm still thinking of exit strategies – rob Malcolm before he forces me to help him commit murder. I pick Riley up. It's a risk, since he might babble something about my exploring to Rachael, but it's better than leaving him here alone.

Also, Rachael told me not to let him upstairs. *"He gets into all sorts up there."* Up the stairs, I find the bedroom. It's a mess, clothes strewn everywhere, make-up stacked on the dresser.

"Bed, bed, bed," Riley sings.

"I see that, sweetheart."

I put him on the mattress, then give it a junkie-quick once-over. It's dusty down under the bed, but thankfully, apart from a couple of plastic containers, there isn't much. The search is quick.

It's just like the old days. My hand comes to rest on a bag duct-taped to the underside of the bedframe. Carefully removing the tape, I slowly bring the package out. Once, I found a bundle just like this, but my hands were shaking and I sliced the bag with my fingernail. Powder fell everywhere, and after, George... well, he wasn't happy about me stealing his drugs.

I stand, staring down at it. Coke, base, a mixture. It's white powder, anyway; it's oblivion. Won't the universe give me a break? I'm standing too close to the bed. And Riley is way too fast and agile for his age.

He reaches up, grabs the bag and then rolls onto the mattress. "Bad, bad, bad," he sings, laughing.

He squeezes the package. The white powder bulges against the plastic. My stomach drops, hard. If even a tiny bit of that gets in his mouth, up his nose...

"Riley, give it here."

He squeezes harder.

# VOLATILE MOODS

I was wrong before, when I said you could've done it well. We both know you would have been a terrible parent. You're far too selfish, or, more particularly, the boundaries of your understanding are far too linked to *you*.

I hate using the N word – narcissist, you degenerate – but sometimes I wonder if it applies to you.

The horror your child would've suffered is unthinkable. Let's be honest.

Sometimes, I try to work out if you would have been outright abusive or, because you'd view the offspring as an avatar of your lofty self, pressure and unfair expectations would've been your weapons. Your volatile moods. Your sudden interest fading as the novelty disappears and you're left with the cold, unglamorous reality of raising a child.

You've never understood real hard work. You've never understood what it takes to truthfully do something *good*. Fine, maybe I don't either. It's not like I'm a force for positivity in the world.

But I *have* done things, some good here and there. Maybe for the wrong reasons and maybe I didn't enjoy it, but I still *did* it.

You've never done a single selfless thing in your life. You like to think you *could* have done some good, if your life had been different – if *I'd* been different – but that's a lie.

You could have had the most perfect life imaginable. You'd still be a monster.

Thank God you've never had children, you idiot. You would've made them as rotten as you. As rotten as me.

# 39

## LORNA

"Are you all right?" Finn asks, glancing over at me as we pull into the driveway.

The closer we got to the street, the more intense the feeling of déjà vu became. I've driven here before, with Malcolm, to see Rachael and her son – from afar. Malcolm was hinting at the box months before the switch.

Hopefully, Rachael doesn't see me. We've never officially met, but Malcolm might've shown her photos. If she does, she'll call me Lorna, and Finn will know something's wrong.

"I'm fine," I tell him.

He smiles tightly across at me. "Is this too weird?"

"No – it's not that."

"Do you want to wait in the car? I shouldn't be long."

"Sure, yes. Thank you."

He climbs from the car, leaving me to twist in my seat and look across the street. There are no cars parked outside her house, but that doesn't mean Rachael's mum isn't in there, taking care of her child.

My leg taps frantically, and I wonder if I should've been religious after all: if the lie I told Sadie makes more sense than the truth. It's like God, or the universe, or fate brought me here, a constant reminder of my old life.

Finn says he won't take long, but five minutes pass with me keeping my head bowed. Another minute, and then a woman walks down the street behind me. She wears a full lime-green tracksuit and has her blonde hair tied up in a messy bun.

She stops at the end of the driveway, then begins pacing, wringing her hands. She glances at the house several times before she spots me, and then she walks aggressively over. Her fist beats against the window.

I close my eyes for a moment, taking a breath. I've been too violent lately. My new life was never supposed to involve any of this. "Yes?" I say, rolling down the window.

"Who are you?" she says, voice slurred.

I aim a tight smile at her, attempting to stay civilised. "L... Sadie." Need to stop doing that. "But, with all due respect, I don't see how that is any of your business."

"You're sitting in my husband's car, love, so it's *definitely* my business."

My head pounds, the madness of the past few days stacking up. "Right."

"So who *are* you? Not your name. What the fuck are you doing hanging around with my man – with my daughter? Huh?"

She slams her hand against the car. If she carries on, this could escalate to a scenario where we might have to ring the police. Which would be bad. "Well?" she demands.

"This has nothing to do with me. Whatever's wrong with you, whatever grudge you have—"

"It's none of your business?" She grins, as if she's just checkmated me, the moron. "Is that what you were going to say?"

I grab the car door, shove it open, thinking of the first time my father hit me, the first time *Malcolm* hit me. I don't have to take this shit, not anymore. She leaps back so the door doesn't hit her.

I spring to my feet, staring coldly. "You're not supposed to be here. Finn's told me about all the shit you're spreading about him. And you're clearly drunk."

With each word, her sneer fills with more meaning; she clearly wants to hurt me. "You don't know what the *fuck* you're talking about." Her voice is too loud.

Rachael should be at work. But it's also possible she's home sick and her car's in the garage, and a scene will bring her out here. She'll see me, the dyed hair, use the name *Lorna*... and maybe Finn will hear.

I step closer, lowering my voice. "If you want anything to do with your daughter, this is the worst thing you could do. You'll never see her again if you carry on. Is that what you want?"

She flinches. "You don't know what your new boyfriend is capable of."

"What did he do – cheat on you, lose all his wages gambling, what?"

These are pedestrian concerns, so disconnected from the mayhem of my life. The murder and the stalking and Elizabeth's video.

"You think you've got it all figured out," the woman says bitterly.

"I just think..." *Fuck*. Over her shoulder, I spot Malcolm's car. I can't see inside the vehicle clearly, but he's got a passenger. It could be Rachael. It could be Sadie. Either one is bad.

"Yeah? What do you think? Enlighten me, *please*."

No time for words, not anymore. Darting my hands out, I grab her shoulders, spin, shove her up against the car. "If you don't leave right fucking now, I'm going to seriously hurt you."

Her eyes snap open. Her toughness drains away.

"I mean it," I hiss. "You're drunk. You're probably high too. How hard do you think it would be to throw you to the ground and kick you in the head?"

I don't enjoy this. Being nasty has never been fun. "Do you

help him?" she whispers, tears in her eyes. "Is that it? You help that sick man to hurt my daughter."

Hurt June? What is Finn doing to her? Off to the side, I see Malcolm's car passing me. "Go. Now."

I give the woman another shove, and she stumbles away.

"Fucking *bitch*," she calls over her shoulder. But she's leaving. That's all I care about.

Quickly, I return to the car, shut the door, keep my head low as I risk a look in the rear-view mirror. Malcolm steps out, Rachael soon after him. They look across the street. I cover my face with my hands.

# 40

## SADIE

R iley grins as he throws the bag in the air and then clumsily attempts to catch it. Every time I get near, he motions as if he's going to tear the bag open. That was my mistake for warning him what would happen if he did that.

*"You're being very bad. You could get yourself hurt."*

That just made it all the more fun, apparently. But the fun ends here. Downstairs, I hear the front door opening, voices raised.

"Lorna?" Malcolm calls.

"Riley. Give it here. *Now.*"

"Bad, bad, bad," he sings.

My nerves are snapping. Vignettes flash across my mind, drugs in every single one, the feeling of powder in my nose. This isn't how I wanted to begin my journey into motherhood, but I don't know what will happen if they come up here to find Riley holding the bag: if they learn I've been snooping.

"If you don't put that bag down," I hiss, "you're going to wake up in the middle of the night, and I'll be standing over your bed, Riley. I'll have a knife in my hand and I'll seriously…"

Oh, thank God. My tone must've been enough. He lets the bag

drop to the bed, and then bursts into tears, throwing his head back and wailing.

I can't afford to think about the fact he's not supposed to be up here, or even spend time thinking of a suitable explanation for why I'm in the bedroom.

Instead, I grab the bag and quickly lie on my side, reaching to the spot where it was taped and replacing it. The tape doesn't stick, the bag falling to the floor. No time. There are footsteps on the stairs.

Leaving it where it is, I stand and quickly grab Riley, holding him to my chest as I rock him. He squirms, attempting to get away from me, my heart cracking right down the middle.

Rachael thunders in through the open doorway like a mother bear ready for battle. "What the hell are you doing up here?"

Malcolm stands at her shoulder, frowning. The look in his eyes is the same from the night he severely assaulted me, the pain of the act lancing through my body in violent memory.

Then he walks into the room. He kneels. He reaches under the bed.

# 41

## LORNA

Finn walks from the house with June in his arms, cradling her to his chest. He aims a warm smile at me, and I do my best to return it. But all I can think about is the fact Malcolm is in the house across the street.

And what June's mother said. About Finn hurting June. Is it true? More importantly, should I give a single *fuck*? I'm only doing this because Elizabeth the crone has given me no choice.

"Buggy, bug, bug," June sings, as Finn arranges her in the car seat.

She reaches out for me, and I turn, offering my hand. She beams as she takes it, drawing my mind to my child, to that night when any hope at being normal was smashed against the wall. When she squeezes my hand, I feel the warm glow of belonging, almost like a taunt. She seems like a happy little girl, but then, so did I when I needed to.

Dad was an expert at forcing me to behave as *truly* happy, non-abused children do. Finn doesn't get into the car right away. He kneels at my side, then stands with a small pin in his hand. He studies it for a few moments, his expression changing to something that makes me think of violence.

A gesture: a nod. He's telling me to get out of the car. With a sigh, I do it, though it's a risk. Just being here is a risk. "What's this?" he asks, showing me a pin with a small flower painted on the front.

I shrug. "How should I know?"

"No – I mean, was Abbey here? That's my ex. Blonde hair. A bit of a mess."

Needing this to be over as quickly as possible, I tell him about the run-in with his ex.

"She was drunk. I told her she had to leave."

"Did you argue?"

"It depends how you define 'argue'. It got a little heated. I told her that if she wanted anything to do with her daughter, showing up drunk and high was the worst thing she could do."

Finn curls his hand around the pin, glancing in the back of the car, at June. "Can I talk to you for a second?" He nods tellingly. He doesn't want June to hear.

He walks toward the street. No, no, no. For *Christ's* sake. Following him, we end up standing in full view of Rachael's house. Her front curtains are open. A quick glance shows me that there are three people in the front room.

Well – four. Malcolm. Rachael, with Riley in her arms. And Sadie. If Malcolm spots me now, the game is over.

"Why do you think it's your place to get involved?" Finn asks, and again, I think of Abbey's words: the accusation that he hurts his daughter.

I didn't believe it a few minutes ago. But studying the angry glint in Finn's eyes, it doesn't seem so ridiculous now.

"I was trying to help."

"You should've sat in the car and ignored her."

"She was hammering on the window. I don't know what else I was supposed to do."

"How about *not* jeopardising my custody by behaving

aggressively toward her? She could make a case for you being a negative influence on June. She could go to the police with this."

"I think you're overreacting."

"Overreacting? She's my daughter! I can't lose her. What's wrong with you? We don't know each other. We're strangers. You're an idiot. You should've kept your mouth shut."

Reality – bleeding. My head – pounding.

"I don't like the way you're talking to me," I say, keeping my voice steady, despite the need to scream right in his sanctimonious face.

"I don't like it when strangers get involved in my business."

"*You* were the one who invited me here. If you thought I was a danger to your daughter – or if Abbey makes that case – it's *your* fault. Anyway, I hear you're the one June should really be scared of."

He inhales sharply through his teeth. I'm familiar with this gesture. I'd never say I've got PTSD, but I've been around enough men to know what it means. He's thinking about all the bad things he could do to me.

We hold eye contact for a long time, waiting for something to happen, then he grunts and turns away. "Enjoy the walk home."

# 42

## SADIE

"So let me get this straight," Malcolm says, tapping his fingernails against the bag of white powder.

It's resting on the arm of the chair, and Malcolm looks *furious*. It's a contained sort of anger. He's not letting himself explode, but I've got no doubt he's going to at some point: maybe here, in front of Rachael and Riley, or maybe at home.

Riley sits on the floor, playing with his dinosaur magnets, the whole scene seemingly forgotten.

"You started snooping around because a *child* told you to?"

The heavy emphasis on *child* makes me think of the threat hanging over my head. The things Malcolm will do to my baby; the things he did to his *own* baby when the birth didn't go as planned.

"I know it was wrong."

Rachael folds her arms. "I told you not to go upstairs."

"You told me *Riley* wasn't allowed up—"

"What difference does that make?" Malcolm cuts in. "You weren't supposed to have anything to do with this. I know you like to pretend I'm some monster, but I never wanted you involved with this shit."

So Malcolm already knew about the drugs, clearly.

"What do we do?" Rachael asks, looking at Malcolm.

She won't meet my eye. It's as if she thinks they're going to have to hurt me in some way, and she can't stand the thought of looking at me beforehand. She needs to dehumanise me.

"That depends." Malcolm's fingers stop tapping, and he leans forward. "Are you going to tell anybody what you found, Lorna?"

"Why would I? It was all a stupid mistake." Even now, the bag calls to me, just like the pills in the box.

"She might be able to help us," Malcolm says, speaking to Rachael as though I'm not even here. "Little Lornie wasn't always such an innocent thing."

The nickname makes me flinch, bringing to mind Rory and Skye.

"We still need to arrange a buyer," Malcolm goes on.

Rachael groans. "I knew we should've got rid of it."

"Why? That's forty grand right there, maybe more. Don't doubt yourself now. Nobody knows you took it, do they?"

Rachael shakes her head. "There were a hundred people in that house, at least. There were at least twenty in the bedroom when I found it. The bloke has been going nuts, demanding to know who took it… but it was what, a month ago? More? I've seen him five times since then, and I don't think he suspects me."

"Good." Malcolm nods. "Lorna's got more experience in the seedy, grimy underworld than you'd think to look at her. Her dad had her scamming people from… how old were you, darling?"

I swallow. Maybe the answer to this was in the journal, meaning it's ash now. It definitely wasn't in the book of facts. Luckily, Malcolm is being rhetorical.

"Since as long as you can remember, right? First, it was the crying scam. Lorna would pretend to be lost, bawling her heart out until some Good Samaritan took pity. Then, when they found her dad, he'd use it to create a connection. A few weeks –

more meetings, dear Daddy whining about a loan he can't pay back. He made a few grand from that."

I don't want to feel pity for Lorna, but I can't help it. My childhood was so much better, my mum showing me love every single day. She'd never force me to do anything like that.

"It was how we met, in fact. Lorna was trying to clone my credit card."

Rachael finally looks at me, gawping, her change of opinion clear in the judgement of her eyes. My opinion is changing, too. So when Lorna lied to me in the beginning, it wasn't a wild gambit. She's a professional.

"But can we trust her?"

"I'm right here," I snap.

"Okay, can we trust you?" Rachael says.

"I'm not going to report you. It's like Malcolm said, I've done too much to judge others. And I understand why you'd want to make some easy money. Riley's a wonderful little boy. He deserves the best life you can give him."

"When you're not making him cry, you mean?"

Malcolm laughs gruffly. "She's got you there. But then, you've never had much of a maternal instinct." The *prick*.

"You'll help us, won't you?" he goes on.

"How?"

"I don't know yet. But when the time comes, you'll do what I ask, won't you?"

A spark in my mind. An idea. I can't keep doing this. But they're right. That bag is worth at least forty grand. Sell it – steal the cash. Start again. No Malcolm and no box.

From the outside, I thought I could tame Malcolm, but that was when I thought he was a run-of-the-mill wife-beater. That was when I thought Jonesy and the others would easily take care of Lorna.

"I'll help in any way I can," I tell him.

"See?" Malcolm claps his hands together. "No reason to

worry. Right. We should get back to work. Lorna, you're still okay with watching Riley until the end of the day."

It's not a question. I nod.

"No more snooping, though." He stands. "Rachael, would you wait in the car for a minute? I need to say something private to Lorna."

Any reasonable mother would scream *no*. She won't leave her child with a woman she clearly doesn't trust: a stranger. But instead, the naïve moron gives Riley a big kiss, a hug, and then leaves. Malcolm leans down, placing his hand on my arm, squeezing. Not hard, but not soft either. "What the fuck were you doing?"

"I don't know. I'm sorry. I'm an idiot."

He lets me go, a sick smile smearing across his face. "You are. But this could also be good for us. We don't just get to have some fun; we'll get the cash too. It's not like she'll have any need for it."

"Bad, bad, bad," Riley sings.

Malcolm scowls at him. "Let's hope our kid isn't as much of a retard as this one, eh?"

I hate that word. And to use it against a child – it's just sick.

"Why did you tell her about my dad?" I ask, hoping for more information.

He chuckles. "Relax. I could've told her what we did to him."

*What did we do?*

"I still remember his face when you sank the knife between his ribs. And what you said after... do you remember?"

I just stare, hoping he'll say it.

"That was the day you fell in love with me," he goes on. "I helped you get rid of the monster who'd tortured you your entire life. Remember that. Remember everything I've done for you."

With that, he leaves, not bothering to hide the bag of white powder. I settle Riley down. He seems to be getting tired, and that's cute to see. Cute to think of the future. Once his eyes are getting heavy, I quickly take the bag upstairs, thinking of the path forward. I wasn't supposed to leave Riley alone. I need to hurry.

I need a plan. Get the money, get away from these people. Protect my baby. And *don't* kill Rachael. It's feasible, but it will mean doing something I really, really don't want to.

# 43

## LORNA

"She thinks he's abusing her?" Elizabeth asks, her words completely at odds with the circumstances.

As soon as I walked into the courtyard, Elizabeth was there, waiting for me. She had an eager look on her face; she'd seen me leave with Finn, apparently, and had seen Finn return alone. Now, we sit in her flat, next to the window, steam rising from her mug of tea. I refused her offer of a hot drink. The less time I spend with this woman, the better. As soon as the video's deleted, I'll leave.

I noticed something interesting a few minutes ago. Elizabeth is wearing a thin shirt. I can see the outline of her bra... and, around her neck, the outline of what looks like a key. It could be a key-shaped pendant of some sort, but if it *is* a key, I wonder if it unlocks her bedside cabinet.

There might be something in there that I could use. But how can I get it? Sure, I could tackle her, wrestle the key away, unlock the cabinet. But if there's nothing inside that helps me, I've given her every reason to use the video.

"Lorna?" she snaps, not such a soft old lady anymore.

"That's what she said. But I'm not sure we can just take her word for it. She was clearly drunk and high."

"And Finn forced you to walk home?"

"Yes."

"What a cruel thing to do."

"He thought I was questioning his ability to be a father."

"So you're defending him?"

"Wouldn't you want me to? He's your son."

"That doesn't mean I condone every bad thing he does. If I'd been around to raise him, he'd never treat a woman with such disrespect. It's a sickening thing to do. But that's men, isn't it?"

"Not all men," I say weakly.

I don't want to agree with the psycho.

"You did well, but now you're going to have to fix it. I need you close to him."

"*You* could easily become friends with him," I say. "He invited me after a short conversation. It's not like I had to convince him. If you pretend to be a nice, generous elderly lady, he'll do the same with you. It won't even be difficult."

"Pretend?" She grins. "Are you saying I'm *not*?"

I need that key; I need some leverage over this hag. I've still got a copy of the key for Malcolm's house. With everything I could steal, plus the money Sadie left for me, I could start a new life somewhere else.

I'm so tired of being involved in the muck of life all the time. Maybe... Hmm, that could work. I need to buy some sleeping pills.

"Put on your sexiest outfit," Elizabeth says. "Go to his flat later. Do all the things men like. Make him believe you're sorry. Make him believe you might have sex with him."

"Why don't *you*—"

"I hardly think I'm his type."

"No – but do what I said. Befriend him. It would be easy."

Especially because Elizabeth is not at all the woman I first assumed. When she speaks, there's this casual fierceness. She reminds me of myself.

"Please don't turn this ugly," she says, after a civilised sip of her tea.

I get it – don't make her blackmail me.

"It might help if I know what exactly you want to learn."

"As much as you can."

"How about this? I'll seduce him this evening. And, when he's asleep, I'll thoroughly search his flat. Every inch of it. His electronics, too, if I can get my hands on them. *But* you have to delete the video tomorrow. Not in a week."

"You'd have to find something special for me to agree to that."

"That's not my problem. I'll do a thorough search, then we're done."

She considers this, and then nods. "That's fair."

"I mean it. This is the deal. You can't go back on it after."

She offers me her hand. "I give you my word." Which could be worthless. But anything which speeds this up is fine with me.

As we shake, I say, "You're being very casual about arranging a hook-up for your son."

"What can I say? I have a unique parenting style."

## 44

### SADIE

I weigh the drugs on Rachael's scales. She has a cooking set that shows percentages of kilograms. It's almost one and a half kilos. Assuming it's coke, then this will be worth at least sixty to seventy grand.

That's enough to start fresh. I won't have the veneer of a respectable life, a husband, a house, the perfect family, blah-blah-blah. But I'll have my baby and freedom, and that's all I cared about to begin with.

"Shall we go for a walk, Riley?" He looks suspiciously up at me, no doubt remembering when I threatened him. God, how sick, a child looking at me that way. But finally, he nods. "We'll go to the park. How does that sound?"

He protests when I put him in the pram, but I haven't got the strength to carry him and I need to get this done quickly, just in case Malcolm makes a surprise visit. He stops babbling when I give him a few dinosaurs to smash together.

Walking down the street with a pram is enough to make me smile, despite the circumstances. This is going to be my life one day, without all the filth that has clung to me for so long.

I've stolen some of Rachael's change so I can use a payphone. Absurdly, I feel guilty. I'll be stealing a lot more than a couple of quid soon.

I type in George's number slowly, the keys cold against my finger. My chest hurts from my pounding heartbeat. I shouldn't let him trigger this terror in me, but it's there all the same. "Speak," he grunts in his usual blunt way.

"It's me."

Dropping the Scottish feels odd.

"I was wondering how long until you came crawling back."

The room – the night – the stink of it... it all returns.

"Have you heard from Jonesy?" he asks when I don't reply. "He disappeared a few days ago. To look for you, I guessed. We'd got word you were in Bristol. But then – nothing. Where is he?"

"I've got no idea," I say honestly, wondering if Lorna's dark side came out. "He's probably high in some den somewhere."

I stand half out of the phone booth, one hand on the pram, pushing Riley back and forth, hoping it brings him some comfort. Or *me* some.

"Seems a bit hypocritical, Sade. It hasn't even been a month since you would've done anything for your next hit. If I told you to tie an old bint to h—"

"I've got a kilo and a half of powder." I can't bear to listen to his sick crap. "That's why I'm ringing. Let's arrange a sale."

"That's funny. I thought you were getting sober."

"I am – I *have*. Almost a month. Are you interested or not?"

"I'm more interested in getting you home. Or arranging a paternity test as soon as we can. We still don't know whose bun you're hiding in your oven."

I swallow, hating this, the truth of his words. It's difficult to breathe. My head is getting hazy. Forcing away the panic, I take a moment, take a breath.

"That's never going to happen," I say. "Anyway, you're not the sentimental type. You don't give a damn if this kid is yours. You've probably got half a dozen kids you don't even know about."

He laughs gruffly. "Fair point. But it's the principle. I can't have my people thinking they can just up and leave anytime they want."

"Well – that's what I've done. I'm not coming home. All I want is to arrange this sale, and then you'll never hear from me again."

"Yeah, we'll see. What are we talking about, anyway?"

"I don't know. Probably coke."

"I need to know if we're going to do this."

"It's not like I can bloody try it! But I can find out." I'll ask Malcolm or Rachael, find a way to slip it into conversation. "I think it's coke, though," I go on. "A friend of mine, he mentioned it has a street value of forty grand."

"That's underselling a kilo and a half."

"I know. But they're not very experienced."

"Oh, Sadie. I'm proud. You're running a little scam, aren't you?"

"Are you interested or not?"

"You know I am. How do we arrange it?"

This is the tricky part. "I need to arrange a few things—"

"Steal the shit, you mean."

"No bullshit. This isn't your chance to get me back."

"I don't care about you *that* much."

I remember the night I left, carrying my pathetic suitcase and a wad of cash to the end of the driveway, George at the window, shirtless, roaring at me that he'd find me and kill me. That was the fate I was going to give to Lorna.

"I'll ring again," I say. "I just wanted to make sure you were interested."

"It must be hard." I can hear the smirk in his voice. "All that lovely powder. You know you could take a small amount without hurting the baby, right? A micro dose. It wouldn't do any harm. Might help with all those nightmares."

"I'm hanging up now."

"Speak soon, beautiful."

I slam the phone in the receiver, way too loud, way too aggressively. Riley starts to cry.

# DRUNK AND HIGH

You showed up to a few of our, let's call them *tête à têtes*, drunk and high.

You were fresh-faced and bright-eyed. I almost assumed it was your youthful vivaciousness making you behave like such a fool. The fall of the fool, that was you, constantly tripping over yourself. When I asked you why, you lied.

You said you just wanted to chill out, take the edge off, a clichéd deceit designed to protect my feelings. Or shield you from my anger, I suppose, if we're going to be *really* accurate about it.

Eventually – after I did some bad things, of which I am honestly not proud – you told me the truth. "I took the shit because my life is shit and it's because of you and, if we're going to do this, then I need some help. Mentally. I don't like it. You *know* I don't like it."

You'd been saying the same thing for a long time, and I was beginning to get tired of it. But there was little I could do. You weren't as pliable and physically vulnerable as you used to be.

I've never been a fan of substances. My parents used them,

and it allowed them to… But that's some woe-is-me nonsense in which I won't indulge.

There are far too many people in this world, whining and complaining about some so-called bad thing that happened to them years ago. And we're all supposed to care, supposed to cry with them, supposed to excuse every bad thing they've ever done.

*Me.*

I've taken action to absolve myself, if that was even necessary. I prove, yearly, I'm not the person I used to be. You'll never change. You don't even try. It's pathetic.

I'm going to tell you that, when I finally do it, watch the life fade from your pretty eyes. I'm going to tell you how worthless you are.

# 45

## LORNA

I wear a shortish skirt, a stylish shirt, and spend a long time on my make-up. I don't want to make my reason for being there too obvious, but I've got to arouse his interest too.

Before I head to his flat, I stow three over-the-counter sleeping pills in my purse. They aren't as strong as the prescription meds, but three should surely be enough to put him to sleep. And for an ancient like Elizabeth... Or I could give her the whole lot. Jam them down her throat and get rid of my problem for good.

That's the solution screaming at me: end her. But for now, I'll go along with her plan.

Finn answers the door shirtless. His hair isn't in its usual braid. It falls in sheets around his face, framing it. He's got more tattoos all over his body, swirling tribals. I wonder if this will be easier because I don't find him physically repulsive.

"Sadie," he says, voice soft. So he's done some thinking about what he did, it seems. Leaving me in the middle of nowhere to make my own way home.

"I've come to say sorry," I murmur, a quiet meek mouse, head bowed. "I shouldn't have gotten involved. It's just – when she started accusing you of being a bad father, I couldn't stand for it. *Anybody* could see what an incredible dad you are."

"Thanks for saying that," he replies. "But *I'm* the one who should be apologising. Do you want to come in?"

"As long as you don't mind?"

He steps aside, waving a hand. "I owe you a hot drink. Well, way more. But it's a start, isn't it?"

I walk into the flat, past June's shoes lined up in the doorway. The living room is covered in toys, as well as two dumbbells with heavy weights stacked onto the ends. There's a faint scent of vanilla, and I notice a candle burning in the corner of the room.

When he returns with the cups of tea, now wearing a shirt, his eyes move over me shamelessly. I spot the hunger in them. He wants me.

I'm here for a reason, I remind myself... and I'm done with men. But I won't lie. It feels good to be wanted by somebody I might actually be able to stomach being with.

"You look great, by the way," he says.

"I had to change. I didn't take money for the bus, so my clothes were all sweaty."

"I'm a complete arsehole, aren't I?"

I take the tea, offer him a flirtatious smile. "You said it..."

"I circled back to get you, for what it's worth. But you weren't there, and I don't have your mobile number."

"Do you want it?"

"I guess it could be useful," he replies, eyes still roaming, lingering on my legs.

Taking out Sadie's phone – *my* phone – I read him the number.

"My memory's terrible," I tell him, when he arches his eyebrow as if to say, *You don't know your own number...* It's a lie. My memory's far too good.

"You were right earlier. I overreacted. After the luck I've had, I should be grateful I've got somebody in my corner."

"Abbey's clearly a terrible mother. I guess she was planning on confronting you. She was drunk and high."

"She's always drunk and high," Finn says. "It's the only reason I've got custody. Courts favour mothers, but not when they show up to hearings with glazed-over eyes and stinking like a brewery."

"She doesn't deserve you... or June."

"I agree on the June front. But I'm not all that special. A binman who can hardly make rent."

"What do you want to do?"

"Tonight?" He smirks. "I can think of a few things."

This is unbelievably forward considering the dick move he pulled on me.

I giggle, sounding absurd even to myself. I'm back to old Lorna, playing a role. "I meant, with your life..."

"I was going to be a musician once upon a time. I play the guitar. But life happened and... well, how many people want to be musicians? It's all right. I'm looking for steadier work. I've got an interview at a fabrication plant tomorrow."

"Good luck." I raise my mug of tea. "I know you'll do great."

"What about you?"

"I'm in between jobs."

"I mean your hopes, your dreams, your wildest fantasies..."

Does this husky-voice, intense-eye-contact thing work on other women? It's not working on me. I can't remember the last time I enjoyed sex. In the early days with Malcolm, perhaps, when the rush of killing Dad hadn't yet turned into the poison of a life spent on the hunt, fulfilling Malcolm's needs.

Yes, *his* needs. No matter what he says to twist my head.

"I'm not sure."

"Come on. Everybody has a dream."

"It's silly."

He stands, walks across the room, sits next to me, bringing the scent of deodorant and heat, bodily warmth that doesn't trigger anything in me. No longing for a different life, one where I can feel all the usual emotions a woman might experience in this situation.

"When I was very young, I dreamed of being a gardener. I used to work in the garden with my mum, when…" *When Dad didn't need me for his 'work'.* "We had the time," I go on. "But I stopped gardening years ago."

I tried, when Malcolm and I first moved in together. But I made too many mistakes while I was learning, apparently; just like his wife, he needed his garden to present a certain image. I failed before he let me make a proper attempt at it.

"Now, I'm not sure. Just a job I can feel a little bit proud of. Maybe care work. I'm still looking."

"You'd make an excellent carer."

I laugh. This one feels more real than my silly schoolgirl giggle. "How can you be sure of that?"

"You're a caring person. You cared enough to stand up for me, when, let's face it, this isn't your fight."

I get the feeling Finn might be a bit of a slut. I've only just apologised – the tea isn't even cold – and he reaches over, laying his hand on my bare knee. He holds it there for a moment, looking at me, probably waiting to see if I'll tell him to get off.

"Where's June?" I ask softly.

"Taking a nap," he says. "She's a very deep sleeper…"

I don't *have* to do this: sleep with him. Even Elizabeth said I only have to make him *believe* I will, to get his defences down, give me a chance to search the flat. So why do I reach down, lay my hand upon his, push so I can feel the heat and the pressure?

Maybe it's because I'm choosing this. For the first time in years, I get to decide.

"Why do I feel like you're hinting at something?" I say.

"Feel free to tell me to go fuck myself…"

He's leaning in. His breath is on my face. Terror grips me. It always does, before the act, but maybe I can finally leave that part of myself behind.

It's not a smart move, leaning in, kissing him, or doing what will come next. It will only make this messier. When I feel his lips on mine, I know I *do* want it. Maybe for the wrong reasons. Maybe it doesn't even have anything to do with him.

Abbey's words cut through me, her accusation: Finn is a bad man who hurts his daughter. She's lying. She has to be.

But what if she isn't? What if I'm about to sleep with another monster? This proves I'm one too, then, because I don't stop him.

## 46

## SADIE

"Her mum's going to come and take over," Malcolm tells me down the phone. "I'm sending a taxi to pick you up." His voice is slurred, and there's an edge to it I don't like. He sounds sick, but also happy about it, like a torturer ramping up to something.

"Where are you?"

"A hotel."

I swallow, my belly hurting. "Why?"

"Silly Rachael had too much to drink. She doesn't want to be alone. We're going to keep her company."

Riley is sleeping now, content in his cot. I study his small, innocent features, experiencing another tightening of my belly. Maybe Rachael is an idiot for stealing drugs from God knows who, and she's obviously naïve, but she doesn't deserve whatever Malcolm is going to do to her.

Or what *I'm* going to do if I don't find a way out.

As the taxi carries me closer, I think about the fact I left the powder at Rachael's place. Stealing it now will only make Malcolm suspicious, but I know where she lives; I can get access to her house just by knocking, smiling, lying.

I have to believe there's an exit strategy, especially when Malcolm texts me.

*Room twenty-one.*

It's too much of a coincidence; that's Finn's flat number. *Another* reason I can't return to my old life, can't continue being Sadie. The universe is head-fucking me. I know a little about Finn. Journalistic whispers from a shade of my old life, a ghostly figure in my mind, one I can't afford to think about.

"Journalism's dead," the receptionist says, mobile held to her ear, then flinches guiltily when she spots me.

"It's okay. I'm meeting someone in room twenty-one."

And I happen to agree. Journalism – death. Jesus Christ, the world is a joke.

———

"Come in."

Malcolm steps aside, weaving on the spot, his eyes bright red and watery. He looks like a far more dangerous version of Rory as he gestures to the bed. Rachael. Passed out. Naked. So far – at least from what I can see – she's unharmed.

"Why isn't she wearing any clothes?" I say quietly, walking across the room.

Malcolm shuts the door and swaggers over, hands on his hips, his work shirt stained with what looks like whisky. Or rusty blood. "Did you bring the coke?"

That's something; I know what the powder is. It hardly seems to matter as I take in the sight of Rachael's chest rising and falling, the stretch marks on her thin hips. "I thought it would be best to leave it behind."

"Hmm." Malcolm shrugs. "Yeah, you're probably light. *Look* at her, though. Fucking perfect. That pussy…"

He keeps going: on and on with the would-be assaulter talk. It's the same stuff I heard from George and the others countless times, describing a woman as a collection of parts, all with a use, but there's nothing worthwhile about the whole. Just the *hole*. I hate these freaks.

"I thought we could make a video," Malcolm says. "Take turns on her."

"Where are her clothes?"

"You a fashion designer all of a sudden?" Malcolm drops onto the edge of the bed, then reaches out and casually begins to stroke his hand along her bare foot. His hand looks so unbearably old against her fish-pale flesh.

This can't happen. Rachael is me, and Malcolm is George and the rest of them, the monsters who take anything they think they can get. But he's done worse. He's *planning* worse.

Fine, all right, I get that. But not here, not now.

"Is she drunk – or drugged?"

"R-Riley?" Rachael mutters in a sleepy voice.

At the same time, Malcolm says, "Just drunk."

A plan forms in my mind. It's risky, but it's the best shot at stopping this. For now, at least. Stepping forward, I glare down at Malcolm. "Are you a fucking moron?"

He laughs at first, but then his features harden.

## 47

## LORNA

We've had sex twice, and it's been unusual. Mostly in the sense that I've actually enjoyed it. I pushed my emotions down for most of it, basically gave myself to the physical sensations, the orgasms and the sweat and the heat and the closeness.

There was *some* emotion, toward the end of the last time, when he was on top and staring at me with so much hunger. It's a new, refreshing feeling: being wanted, and the man caring if I'm enjoying it.

But it doesn't change what I have to do. When he returns from reading June her bedtime story, I remind myself that this is the man who left me in the middle of nowhere, with no cash to buy a bus ticket.

I have to remember that. Otherwise I'll feel guilty about the glass of orange juice sitting on his side of the bed. *His* side, as if we're a couple.

"Are you trying to seduce me?" He smirks as he sits on the bed, picking up the glass. With his other hand, he reaches over and caresses my arm. "Seriously, thank you."

"It's just a glass of orange juice, relax."

He necks the whole thing, then grins. "It's the most delicious, most perfect glass of orange juice I've ever tasted."

"Will you hold me?"

He lies on the bed, and I lay my cheek against his heart, telling myself it's so I can listen to the beating slow down, signalling unconsciousness, and begin my search. The sex was good, but this – the so-called intimacy – is nothing but a trick. Eventually, his hand relaxes. His breathing gets heavier.

I wait a few more minutes, and then slowly slip out of his grasp and stand up.

# 48

## SADIE

Malcolm has been staring at me for a long, long time. It feels like it could be a minute, maybe two, and I've been doing my best to hold his gaze. If this plan is going to work, I can't show any fear, for even a second.

"Explain," he finally says, tightening his hold on Rachael's foot.

She moans softly in her sleep, but she doesn't wake; she doesn't comment on the fact my *husband* stripped her while she was sleeping.

I step forward, glaring down at him. "Did you book this hotel in your name?"

"Yes."

"And people saw you come up here together."

He sighs heavily. "They did."

"And your plan is to *assault* her? And to record her? How much did you drink today? This is the most idiotic thing I've ever heard."

"Careful…"

He tries to stand, but then he drops back to the mattress, too drunk even for that. I don't have to fake my disgust, just the reason.

"I thought you were serious about the box. I thought you were ready for this. But clearly, you're not. This is *amateur*, Malcolm. This is the most stupid thing you could've done, honestly."

"Enough."

I know what happens next. It's difficult not to smooth my hands over my belly, but that would project weakness. He's waiting for that. More staring, then he lowers his gaze.

"Maybe you're right. This is the sort of thing that could get us caught. In the long run, it'll be better to leave her here, won't it?"

"We have to get her home," I tell him.

Her son will miss her, little Riley with his mischievous nature.

Malcolm sighs. "All right, fine. But you do it. I'll wait here."

"Where are her clothes?"

He grunts, gesturing to the corner of the room. He's shoved them all under the small desk. I grab them, and then go to Rachael, softly nudging her shoulder.

"Rachael, I'm going to help you get dressed, all right?"

She murmurs wordlessly. She's really out of it.

But this isn't the first time I've dressed an unconscious person. I had friends in my old life, or *near* friends at least, women who vomited on their own clothes and then passed out. I'd feel rare moments of pity, and do what I'm doing now: carefully manoeuvre their bodies until they were dressed.

"Rachael," I say, louder, close to her ear. "You have to help me. I'm taking you home? Okay?"

"Y-yeah," she says, her eyes peeling open. "Where am I?"

"A hotel room. You needed to lie down. I think you drank too much."

"Hmm." She nods, seeming so young it hurts. I help her to her feet, and she clings onto my arm. "Where's Riley?"

"At home. You'll see him soon."

"O-okay. Malcolm?"

She looks around the room. Malcolm's sitting in the corner, at the desk, but he's turned the chair so he's facing us. "Go home, Rachael, before you embarrass yourself anymore."

A look of complete shame captures her features. She truly believes she's the one in the wrong.

"I'll need money for the taxi," I say.

Malcolm reaches into his pocket, then basically throws his wallet at me. "Hurry up."

Outside, I open the wallet. As Rachael leans against the wall, I rifle through, wondering what the limit on his two credit cards are. I check every pocket. Something's folded up in the zip section, wedged deep. It's probably a receipt, but I check it anyway. I gasp, causing Rachael to spin around and stare at me. "What's wrong?"

"Nothing," I whisper.

But that's a lie. It's a photo of Mum, our *birth* mother, not Olivia. She's sitting in the hospital bed, a tired smile on her face, a baby in each arm. I've seen this photo before. I had my own copy before the switch, before I burned it so Lorna wouldn't find it.

I can't think of a reason why she would give a copy to Malcolm. Or why or how they would've met.

"Lorna," Rachael says.

"Yeah?"

"Can you please take me home?"

She clings onto my arm, and I quickly shove the photo back into the wallet.

## 49

## LORNA

I walk quietly through the flat.

The fear is far less than I'd experience if I was sneaking around behind *Malcolm's* back. I don't expect Finn to launch into a night-long torture, during which he'll indulge every perverse fantasy that's ever entered his damaged mind.

I search the kitchen first, opening every drawer. Protein shakes, sweets for June, tins of spaghetti and the usual detritus of life. There are no secret notes, nothing indicating hidden darkness. Under all the counters; on top of them.

I move to the living room, going through the same routine, until I come across a sticky note pressed right to the back of the drawer in the TV cabinet, folded four times. It has a seemingly nonsensical string of letters and numbers written on it.

*Xop2120!1xwdlD*. A password, clearly.

Taking a photo of it on my phone, I return it to its original place. There's nothing else in the living room; the bathroom is similarly bare. Unless Elizabeth considers a half-empty tube of toothpaste of interest.

I can't search June's room. There's too much of a chance she'll wake up. Returning to the bedroom, I find Finn on his side, his arm propped beneath his head. He's snoring loudly, but I'm careful as I stalk across the room anyway.

The sex stink causes sickness to churn in my belly, though I don't regret what we did. But the smell always provokes this response, since it's usually associated with Malcolm. Finn's laptop sits closed on the small corner desk. I walk carefully to it, glancing at him every few moments, and then sit down and open it.

I expect the password, but it's a four-digit pin. Dammit.

I spin quietly in the chair, looking around the room for possible hiding places. But he'd have no reason to write down, then hide, a four-digit pin. Even the most forgetful person imaginable could remember that.

An idea occurs to me. Finn's phone is on the bedside cabinet. He moans sleepily as I approach, then one eye peels open and he seems to stare up at me. *Seems* to, because he's still passed out, but the white of his eye makes me feel seen.

A new beginning, yeah, right... I'm back to the same old crap. His phone has face ID, so I swipe then hold it to his face, hoping the illumination of the screen doesn't jolt him awake. I'm in.

Going to his calendar, I swipe through the months, stopping whenever there's an event on one of the days. There are several bank holidays, a few notes for job interviews, and finally, his birthday. I remember the date, then find June's birthday too.

Since I'm already on the phone, I search every program and app. I haven't got time to go through all his conversations – these sleeping pills aren't *that* strong, after all – but there aren't any photos or videos that Elizabeth would find...

What? Useful? Insightful? I'm not even sure what she thinks she's going to get from this. Back to the computer, I try his birthday as four digits. It fails, but when I try June's, the laptop slowly begins to log in, the circular buffering symbol moving around and around. The laptop has a cluttered desktop with a seemingly random assortment of programs.

Finn stirs behind me, moaning softly. I half close the laptop, wait, watching as he rolls over and buries his face in the pillow.

Once he's settled, I start searching, going to the folder list and clicking through them one by one. There are several CVs, a half-written letter to June's mother (mostly containing swear words), a few photos of a dog in a folder marked *Pepper*.

And then another folder, titled *Boring Finance Stuff*. If I've learned anything about human nature, it's to *always* look at the so-called boring stuff. The folder contains one program, *LockSafe*. When I click it, a password window appears.

I type in the code I found on the sticky note. A window pops up. Dozens of photos... *hundreds*, maybe more.

I stare, teeth gritted, head aching. It's like I can feel my womb trying to crawl out of my body so it can instantly decay and die. That sounds like the ramblings of a madwoman, but that's the regret I feel at sleeping with this man.

It hurts to do this, but Elizabeth will need proof. I take a photo of the screen, then turn off the laptop.

Walking into the kitchen, I grab a knife, struggling to control my breath. I let this *animal* inside of me. Returning to the bedroom, I stow the knife under the bed. I won't hesitate if I have to use it. But I can't leave, either. It's important I pretend everything is normal.

He wraps his arm around me, groaning, pushing his face against the back of my neck so I can feel his hot, ugly breath tickling down my spine.

## 50

## SADIE

"I think she's had a little too much to drink," I tell Rachael's mother.

She stands in the hallway, hands on her hips, the lines in her face deepening as she takes in the sight of her daughter. Rachael is a little more sober now, but she still has to cling onto my arm to stay upright.

"With your son sleeping upstairs," Annabelle says, scowling. "Christ, Rachael."

"I don't know what happened," Rachael says, and I wince.

She can't start speaking like that. It could lead to questions, which will lead back to Malcolm. If our life erupts before I find a way out, I'm screwed. Somehow, I doubt Lorna is going to want to switch back. If I was her, I wouldn't, especially because she's been able to avoid George and the others for now.

"Let's get you to bed," Annabelle says, and then Riley starts to scream from upstairs.

"My baby," Rachael moans.

Annabelle holds up a manicured finger. "You're in no state to see him."

"I can take her to bed," I tell Annabelle.

Without another word, she turns and strides up the stairs, taking them two at a time. She stomps like Mum used to when she was angry – Olivia, not the woman in the photo, the woman who lives in Malcolm's pocket. No time to think about that now.

"Am I a terrible mother?" Rachael slurs as I help her up the stairs.

"No," I lie.

But really – stealing drugs, abandoning her child at every opportunity, with a *stranger* too... All I know is, I'm going to do my best to be the complete opposite of her when it comes to my child.

"Except for the coke," I say, when we reach the landing, my voice purposefully just a little too loud.

Rachael looks sharply at Riley's bedroom door, then glares at me. "Shh."

"Sorry, but it's a really, *really* silly thing to do. If you're caught with that amount, you'd do real time. Riley wouldn't have his mother. He'd hate you for abandoning him."

She crumples, the tears starting. It doesn't feel good to make her cry. "It was a stupid thing to do," she whimpers. "I've always done stupid things. I can't help it. It's just who I am."

"Shh, don't say that." Leading her into her bedroom, I sit her on the bed and stroke her hair. "But Riley has already seen the drugs, obviously."

"Because you let him," she says bitterly, struggling to sit upright.

"No – he's the one who *led* me to them. So he must've seen them before."

She paws at her face. "I didn't mean for him to. He's so capable for his age." The pride in her voice almost derails me. It's too sincere, too full of genuine love. As if I didn't already feel like a bully.

"Why don't you let me take it for you?" I say. "You won't have to worry about it then."

"But I need the money."

"Don't worry. You'll still get your share." I'll decide if this is true later.

"Maybe next time, Riley will sneak in there and tear the bag open. He doesn't know what it is. He'll be curious, eat some, then maybe…"

"Please, stop."

"Do you want your son to OD?"

"N-no."

I could've just stolen it, but this is better. It means I won't have to deal with Rachael's accusations or any fallout from the theft.

"Don't worry," I whisper, touching her shoulder tenderly as she lies on her side. "Everything's going to be okay."

"Malcolm wouldn't steal from me," she murmurs, half asleep.

"No, of course not."

"He loves his son," she goes on. "I know he does."

I don't care, obviously. Malcolm can have dozens of children, but it would be yet more evidence of how inhuman he is, choosing the mother of his child as his next victim. Rachael smiles, but there's nothing happy about it. She looks ill. "I'm sorry. I wasn't supposed to tell you…"

"It's all right. I already knew. And you're right. Malcolm loves him."

"I knew it."

Stowing the coke in my handbag, I resolve to get as far away from him as quickly as possible. If he's willing to do this to Rachael, when she's already given birth to his child, he'd do far worse to me.

# STEAL AND LIE AND CHEAT AND HURT

It's easy to steal and lie and cheat and hurt when you realise – when *one* realises; I'm not sure you ever needed an epiphany, since you always knew this – that some people are simply not worth as much as others.

It's a cruel thing to say, to think, but it's the truth.

Walk down any high street in the country and you'll see countless people who might as well not be breathing.

Fat toddler-like men with superhero logos on their T-shirts vaping with one hand and swiping their phone with the other. Or women without personalities, but with pins on their bags, a new hairstyle, stupid punky earrings, anything to convince themselves they exist, they're real.

Log into Facebook and read some of the things people post. Shameless pointlessness, offering nothing to the world. *Are you okay, hun? PM me, hun.*

Morons, most people. I happen to agree with the Marquis de Sade; some people are disposable for the pleasure and enjoyment of others.

Sometimes, in extremely rare moments, I'm jealous of the regular person.

Sometimes – again, *rarely* – I imagine what it would be like for my only thoughts to be what television programme I was going to watch next, a new type or flavour of gin, some pointless non-story about how the bus driver made a rude comment or whatever nonsense people blabber about.

Then, later, I hate myself for ever wanting to be like them. Fuck them all. I can do whatever I want to them, whenever I want. Not to sound egotistical, but compared to them, I'm God.

# 51

## LORNA

"Sadie?" Finn says sleepily, at around three in the morning.

I haven't slept for a moment, lying frozen next to him – this man I'd happily wrap in a rug and drive out to the countryside, toss him in the dirt next to Jonesy, where he belongs.

"Hmm?" I murmur, pretending to be asleep.

"I'm knackered. What time is it?"

"I'm not sure. It feels late." I make my voice tired, the syllables drawn out. "I guess we got carried away…"

He chuckles, then lays his hand on my hip, squeezing as if he's tempting me to grab the knife from under the bed, drive it into his throat, lacerate until he's choking and bleeding and dying like the pig he is.

"You can say that again. I'm going to go and check on June."

No – he can't. The poor girl. Just like me, with Dad, and all the things he did. All the stuff I'll never look at, not completely. And maybe it triggered some darkness in me, agony I vented in unnatural and unhealthy ways. And maybe it will do the same to June. Pain begets pain begets pain.

"All right." I sit up. "I'm going to head home, anyway."

"Are you sure?" he asks, standing up and walking around the bed. "You don't have to… I was thinking round three, maybe?"

I can't believe that smirk ever did anything for me, sexual or otherwise. "I'd love to. But really, I've got an early start."

He sighs, shrugging. "Fair enough."

"I'll let myself out."

He turns away, and I wait until I hear June's bedroom door open. Quickly getting dressed, I tuck the knife into the waistband of my trousers and then leave the flat. I can't risk replacing it now, too many questions if he catches me.

I don't go home. Instead, I hurry upstairs to Elizabeth's flat. I knock urgently, the knife handle pressing reassuringly into my hip, as if protecting me from the photo on my phone: the countless photos on Finn's laptop.

Elizabeth pulls the door open, wearing a baggy nightie that makes her seem older, thinner. And somehow more threatening, as if she's all sharp edges. "Sadie, it's late," she murmurs.

"I did what you asked."

"And?"

"Your son's a paedophile."

She steps aside, gesturing into the flat. "You better come inside."

---

We sit in her living room, the lamps lit, her legs folded. There's something different about her from the first time we met, as though she's dropped any pretence at being a kind, scared old lady. There's something savage in her expression, but I can't figure out exactly what.

"Delete the video," I tell her.

"You've been too useful to me," she says.

"We had a deal."

"What did you see, exactly?"

I explain about the folder on Finn's laptop, then take out my phone, open the photo, and slide it across the table. Elizabeth picks it up, then drops the phone right away.

"That was on your son's computer. So any dreams you had at building some perfect, lovey-dovey relationship... any dreams that you were going to reconnect, find common interests, any of that – let them go."

"This must be a mistake," Elizabeth murmurs. "You need to keep searching. Or get him drunk. Yes, that could work. Get him drunk an—"

"We're *done*," I interrupt. "I did what you asked."

"But I didn't expect this. I need more time."

"Then do it yourself. There are countless ways you could ingratiate yourself with the freak."

"I'm not deleting the video."

I sit back, looking at the key hanging around Elizabeth's neck. I can see the outline, and I remember when I searched this place, the locked bedside cabinet. Surely, that's what the key is for. I've still got some sleeping pills in my pocket.

"Cup of tea?" I ask.

"Ah, so British." Elizabeth smiles, almost sadly. "Nothing is truly unfixable when you introduce tea into the equation."

I go into the kitchen, making sure the mugs are out of view of the divider, then discreetly reach into my pocket and take out a few capsules. Opening them, I pour the powder into the mug on the left; they're identical, yellow with little roses on them. Returning to the living room, I place them on the coffee table.

"Are you angry with me?" Elizabeth asks.

"It's hard not to be, honestly. You gave me your word."

"Things are more complicated now."

"Not for me."

Elizabeth picks up her tea, sniffs it. What is she, a bloody canine? Her nose wrinkles, and I'm sure I'm busted. She's somehow smelled me out. "Is there sugar in this?"

"You can *smell* when there's no sugar, can you?"

She laughs harshly. "I'll take that as a no. Would you like any?"

"No, thank you."

She carries her mug into the kitchen, stirs in the sugar, then returns.

"You have to understand my position," she says. "I've spent so long dreaming about this. My son. My baby boy. And now you're telling me he takes photos of my granddaughter. It's… I can't take it."

"It's the truth. How do you think I feel? I slept with the pervert."

Elizabeth lays her mug down without taking a sip, looking around the room.

"When I first moved in here, I imagined reconnecting with Finn. I imagined bonding, and – it's silly. But I thought we'd all take a trip one day, nowhere especially special. But a family thing. And I'd hang a photo there."

She nods to an empty section of the wall, next to the window. It would be a good spot for a photo, it's true, not that I care.

"Do you still want that, after what I've showed you?"

"I'd be insane if I did, wouldn't I?"

"Yes. You would."

She sighs, finally sipping her tea. I do the same, hoping to hurry her along. It doesn't take long for me to realise my mistake. When I was staring at the wall, the possible spot for the photo, she switched the drinks. My eyelids get heavy.

190

# 52

## SADIE

I lie next to Malcolm, questions burning in my mind. About his baby with Rachael, about when I'll be able to arrange the drug deal. Most of all, I think about the photo I found. When did she find him? Why?

"What's wrong with you?" he grunts.

I lie still. "I thought you were asleep."

"Can't when you're kicking me every two bloody seconds."

This is a mistake, but I have to know. The journalism, the pain, the blood, the regret, and blocking it all out, most of all: pour powder on it, inject liquid into it, blot it, bury it.

"I found a photo in your wallet. Of a woman holding two babies. I didn't recognise her."

He sits up. We're still in the hotel room. I guess Malcolm didn't want to waste it. "Snooping, were you?"

"Looking for change," I say quickly.

"Shouldn't have given you the damn thing. But that's booze for you."

At least Lorna didn't already know about this. I've just realised – too late – I could've sabotaged myself by telling him I didn't recognise her.

"She's nobody," he says after a pause. "Nobody *you* need to worry about, anyway."

"I think it's fair for me to worry about my husband carrying around photos of other women." My voice is far too harsh, but I can't help it. It's the memories the photo provokes. The hate of it all.

"You think I'm screwing that old hag?"

"Then why keep her photo?"

"Lorna…"

He rolls over, strokes his hand over my belly. I expect there to be a threat in his touch, but it's surprisingly tender. It could be fake; it probably is. But it's preferable to anything else he offers.

"You don't need to hear this. It's all crap. And anyway, I sent her away."

I freeze up next to him. "What does that mean?"

He sits up, removing his hand from my belly, his sigh somehow volcanic. "It doesn't matter."

"It does to me."

"She's your mum. Not the demented hag rotting in a home. Your birth mum. Just after we arrived in Weston, she showed up. She wanted to meet you, she said, wanted to get to know you better. I told her to leave, said some pretty vicious stuff about what I'd do if she came back."

I say nothing, mind spinning. So this was after the journalism, after I ran and fell into a pit of oblivion. "Why did you keep the photo?" I ask after a pause.

"She begged me to give it to you. I don't know why, but I kept it, thought maybe I might. Then time passed and it didn't seem so important. Are you angry with me?"

I almost snort out a laugh. As if I could be honest about that. "No, I understand why you didn't say anything."

He grunts; the topic is over. What would be a cup-throwing day-long war of an argument for any other wife, is a nothing for Lorna, instantly deflated.

"While we're sharing home truths," he goes on. "I've been thinking about Rachael. Maybe it's you being pregnant. Maybe it's... I don't know. But I think we should choose somebody else."

"Is that because Riley is your son?"

He laughs grimly. But there's still no threat, no tightening of the hand. Then he hugs me, kisses the top of my head. I cringe even as a pathetic part of me seeks the comfort: not from him, the *real* him, but the man he's pretending to be. If he pretends for long enough, could I accept it?

"He's nothing to me, but the lad could do with keeping his mother. Tomorrow, I'm going to book an appointment for you and the little bairn, make sure everything's in tip-top shape."

*Where is this coming from?* But I can't say it. I might shatter whatever spell has taken hold of him. "That would mean so much to me," I say, thinking of the assault, the violence, the possible damage.

"I bet you're wondering where Malcolm the monster has gone, eh?" This could be a trick. I can't say yes. "Be honest," he snaps.

All right, dammit. "Maybe a tiny, tiny bit."

"I've decided to be a good boy. You see, all those bad feelings, all that anger, all the shame, I'm going to do my best not to aim it at you anymore. I've got a different target."

"Oh?"

"You're going to find me someone else. And then, when we... do what we do, I'll aim it all at her instead. For you and the baby, I'm going to be a good man."

What an insanely deluded statement. He's going to grotesquely torture and murder an innocent girl, but with us, he's going to be *good*, whatever that can possibly mean for him. There's some darkness in me. If I can just believe hard enough...

"I have to tell you something," I say.

"Yeah?"

"I took the coke from Rachael's house."

He kisses the top of my head again. This can't be happening; there can't be a shimmer around my shoulders, a tempting tease. This man assaulted me not that long ago. *Get it together, Sadie.* It's just like with George, so grateful to be treated with the smallest dignity.

"That's good. But we'll need to figure out how to sell it."

"I've been looking into that online," I tell him.

"Using our computer? Are you stupid?"

"I used a VPN, and the Tor Browser."

"What does that mean?"

"It hides us. Nobody can see what I'm doing."

He laughs, and there's *real* warmth in it now. "Clever. How did you figure that out?"

George taught me; using the dark web was a small part of his druggie business. "Just research. But I might be able to arrange a sale."

"Do it," he says. "And let me know if you need my help. It feels good, doesn't it, working together?"

I want to say no. But, as wrong as it is, yes, it does feel good. Or at least better than the alternative.

# 53

## LORNA

I open my eyes, the world blurry, just about making out the silhouette of a gargoyle bent over a bedside cabinet, pulling at it with its claws, gawping at me over its shoulder.

My vision clears, and I see Elizabeth standing in the lamplight. She's bending down so she can slot the key into the lock without removing it from her necklace.

"I suppose your head must be aching quite terribly," Elizabeth says.

"Yeah," I say, my forehead splitting, my mouth dry.

"The drugs. And I bumped you getting you in here. It's a difficult task for an older lady."

I move to stand up, then the ropes cut into me. I'm tied to a chair, wrists bound behind my back, shoulders arched in an unnatural angle from the position. My legs are tied too. "What are you doing?" I ask, when she opens the drawer and takes out what could be a barber's set, a small leather satchel.

She opens it on the bed. Knives gleam at me, sharp tools, catching the lamplight. Then she takes out some plastic wrapping, duct tape, objects of murder and disposal. I'm struggling to breathe as I stare at the objects, one by one, and I know I judged this woman completely wrong.

"You tried to drug me, silly girl," Elizabeth says, frowning as she takes a knife from the satchel.

"I could scream."

"You could. But we both know that would be a mistake."

"Why – because you'll kill me?"

"So we're asking silly, obvious questions now, are we?"

She tosses the knife from hand to hand with surprising agility. When she comes closer, I try not to squirm. I try. "Why did you slip that little something into my drink, Lorna?"

"Because I wanted to delete that video. Or find something to blackmail you with. It's not complicated." She tilts her head at me, grinning strangely, as if I'm missing something.

"You called me Lorna."

"Ta-da." Elizabeth laughs, sitting on the edge of the bed, holding the knife in one hand as she reaches over with the other, placing it on my knee. "You really are an excellent actress. Your father taught you well. Not your *birth* father. He was a… well – a bad man. The less said about him, the better. But the man who adopted you, he really did teach you well."

I spit in her face. "He abused me. Sexually, physically, everything on the bloody list." She wipes the spit from her face, but I keep going, my panic constricting my throat. "He was a monster. He deserved what he got."

"You murdered him. You and Malcolm. I'm proud of you. My daughter – a strong, capable girl."

I struggle to breathe, to talk. Painfully, I'm not even surprised. This was the connection I felt. "If that's what you think…"

She shrugs. "It only makes sense. I've watched you and Malcolm over the years. I tried to make contact a while ago, but he told me to back off, and he seemed serious. Malcolm watches women and girls. I'm assuming you know that. He'll go to bars and watch students drinking, follow them from bar to bar. Sometimes, he'll fuck one. I can see none of this is news to you."

I don't show any reaction. My knee tingles as her touch tightens.

"A regular person would think, perhaps, he's in the early stages of voyeurism. But I'm seasoned in these things. I knew the look on his face. I could read the *practical* hunger in his posture. Or perhaps it was because I'd already looked into your past. Faraday, the other girls, the suspicion. Nothing ever proven, but wherever Malcolm goes, a girl or two goes missing. It's impressive."

"Impressive? It's sick. It's wrong. He should've been caught by now."

"Ah, sweet girl," Elizabeth says. "You can't lie to your mother."

My *mother*? She's playing more games. She has to be. And yet, deep down, it rings viciously true.

"My mother is rotting in a home in Scotland, completely demented. Where she belongs. *You're* not my mother."

"You came from my body. You and Sadie. We're one and the same. I saw you that night, when I found you with your little corpse friend. Before you remembered how you were supposed to feel. There was a thrill, wasn't there? Excitement? Passion?"

I twist away.

"I've felt the same," she whispers, placing both hands on my knees now; she's dropped the knife. "Many times. It's sad, how repetitive life can be. What happened to you, at the hands of your father, much the same happened to me. It must be far more common than people think."

"Or we're unlucky."

She sighs. "Yes – or that. So I took a path remarkably similar to yours. Well, to begin with. But somewhere along the way, you started to help *him* hurt women. What was it, payment for dispatching your father, simple fear?"

"Maybe a mixture of the two," I say, hoping she can't hear the emotions in my voice.

"But when it came to your father and that other man, the one we buried together, you felt a thrill, didn't you, Lorna?"

"You need to answer some questions," I say, while ignoring hers.

She sits back, spreads her hands. "At least you're willing to look at me. It became too much for dear Sadie, what I am. She hates me. *Hates* me. She thinks she's so much better. Even after everything I've done to help her. Like get her a flat, for one – *your* flat now, I suppose. I helped her escape those drugged-up animals, and she *still* can't bear to look at me."

Elizabeth grits her teeth, and I get a preview of how she must look when she's on the hunt.

"I'll answer anything," she says.

"Okay. Good. Fine." Let's test the bitch. "Why did you give us up for adoption?"

"I wasn't fit to be a mother. I didn't want you." It shouldn't hurt, but somehow, impossibly, it does. "When and why did you reconnect with Sadie?"

"This feels like a job interview." Elizabeth idly toys with the knife. "I always imagined it would be more emotional."

"I'm tied to a fucking chair."

"I found Sadie before I ever found you. I've made certain contacts over the years. Technically, I was – and still partly am – a journalist. A traveller who focuses on human-interest stories. It helps in my other *work*, shall we say. Anyway, I found Sadie just after her mother passed. I reached out, and then... well, I discovered she wasn't like me."

"Explain."

"So blunt."

"Just tell me."

"Sadie has never been very good with money. She was living off her inheritance, but not working. Apparently, she was thinking of studying English literature. *Thinking* of studying it... but in the meantime, doing nothing except going out with her friends and reading books."

"What does that have to do with murder?"

Elizabeth beams. "See – she'd never say anything like that, so frankly, to me, while tied to a chair. You're the same, so similar, and yet one's a devil, one's a saint."

"Sadie's no saint. She tricked me into switching."

"But you didn't believe her."

"How do you know that?"

"Because you're far more similar to me than Sadie ever was, or will ever be, and I wouldn't have been fooled. I showed her my work, my *real* work, but she insisted on calling it journalism. I won't lie, things got a little... uneasy at the end. But I wanted her to *see*."

"Uneasy, how?"

"Oh, that's enough about her." Elizabeth gestures with the knife, her calm cracking. "All I care about is this – are you going to help me, or get in my way? You're the daughter I've always wanted, and now, that other *girl* has done me a favour. She's removed Malcolm from the equation. We're free to work together."

"To do what?"

Elizabeth stands abruptly, then walks closer with the blade – there's a moment when I'm convinced she'll kill me – and then she leans down, cutting the ropes around my wrists. I massage the raw skin.

"To get rid of Finn. He's not my son, by the way."

"No shit, Sherlock."

She grins as she leans down, cutting the ropes around my ankles. "He's my next target. I learned about his filth via a dark-web watchdog I subscribe to – under an alias, of course."

"Of bloody course."

Elizabeth grins up at me. "Sadie cried when she learned who I was. She hugged me. She really broke down." I stare at her. "But you're not Sadie, are you, cherub?"

"What are you going to do to Finn?"

"You saw sexual photos of his own daughter and other little girls on his computer, correct?" I nod. "Then I'm going to make him pay. But we've got to be careful. I don't want him getting in the way of our other target. Our dream target."

"Who?" She gives me another look, and then, miraculously, I find myself smiling. "Malcolm," I whisper.

"I was testing you. Pretending not to know who you were. You showed me how tough you are. What you did to that man… a little amateur, but vicious, effective. And breaking into my flat. I'm proud."

"You are?"

She takes my hands. "You're ready."

## 54

## SADIE

"Doesn't it feel real now?" Malcolm smiles as he reaches from the driver's seat, placing his hand on my belly.

We've been to the hospital this morning. It was my first time in a private hospital, like entering a shiny new world, the nurses and doctor treating me more like a celebrity than a patient.

The baby's fine, apparently. Everything seems all right. We're in the system. *Lorna* is officially pregnant.

"It does," I agree.

I did a few tests before, but I didn't go to the doctor, and what with the violence and the stress... But there's no need to worry about that anymore. Not the violent part, anyway. Hopefully.

"What are your plans for the day?" he asks. "Does it involve... the bag of fun powder? Or perhaps a certain young lady..."

"Do you have anybody in mind?" I ask, a pit opening in my stomach and swallowing all the positive emotions. Not that there should've been any to begin with. I can see how Lorna became institutionalised to the madhouse of this prick's moods.

"I'm sure you'll find somebody suitable," he says. "I'll want photos soon. See what she looks like. And let me know when there's an update about the powder. I'm starting to feel like a criminal mastermind."

He laughs, sits back, nods for me to climb out of the car. I'm not sure if Lorna knows what Malcolm does when he's not at work. But during my short time following him, I saw him daytime drinking, alone. Or going to betting shops. Anything except being with his wife. Since he's already pulled a sickie and he's driven me home, maybe he's going to reward himself. Which is all he does anyway.

Behind him, Lorna appears. She's wearing my black, torn jeans and a goth-esque hoodie. Malcolm starts to turn, probably wondering what I'm staring at, so I grab him, both hands clasping his face, and kiss him more convincingly than I've ever kissed anyone.

He groans, kisses me back, then gives me a soft nudge when I place my hand on his leg.

"You're going to be a mother. Act like it, not a slut."

Lorna's gone. Thank God. I don't know how we'd ever explain that.

"I'm sorry," I say, climbing from the car.

---

A few minutes later, after Malcolm leaves for work, the doorbell rings. It's Lorna, with her hood up now, tightened so it shadows her eyes.

"What are you doing?" I grab her arm and pull her inside.

She shrugs me off, striding in like she owns the place. "We need to talk. Mummy paid me a visit." We have a standoff in the hallway.

"She told me some interesting things. Like apparently you and she went on a little murder tour. You called it *journalism*. Ring any bells?"

"Where is she now?" I ask, expecting a hand over my mouth any second.

"She's living in your building," Lorna says, so smug, tossing her head as she pulls her hood down. "Quite the dramatic place, that sad-as-fuck block of flats. But you know that already. She's the one who helped you escape your little druggie friends."

"Yes, but I mean – now, right now? Where is she?"

"Not here," Lorna says. "Do you mind if I make a cup of tea?"

I follow her into the kitchen. "It was stupid, showing up here."

Her words have triggered far too much darkness in me, pain I'd rather not look at, never have to think about. It threatens to erupt to the surface as I watch my double gliding around the kitchen with ease.

"I know what the box is," I tell her.

Her shoulders tighten, but only for a second. Then she begins to hum along with the sound of the kettle. "Would you like one?"

"You've helped him kill countless women."

"Not countless." Lorna turns, looking like a guilty kid, as if her crimes are so much lesser than they are. "And he *forced* me. Anyway, you'll be doing the same now. Why was he here this morning?"

"Hospital, for the baby."

"Oh, look at you." She smirks. "You're beginning to enjoy this new life, huh?"

"Not so much. Why are *you* here?"

"Mummy tied me to a bloody chair. She told me some interesting things. So I'm here to warn you... get away from Malcolm."

"You told me that before."

"I really mean it this time. This is the last time I'll say it."

Bright, ugly images in my mind, rancid stinks, the bloody blunt reality of what happened. "Has she chosen Malcolm?"

Lorna shrugs with a coy smile. "Chosen him for what?"

"You can't trust that woman." I slam my hand on the counter, a jolt crushing up my arm. "The first time we met, she told me she was going to take me along for some *journalism* work. The bitch took me to a weird BDSM club and forced me to watch a man getting beaten until his back bled. A test, she said."

"You must've been soft if you couldn't watch that."

I lay my hand on the not-yet-a-bump. "I am not soft."

*"Oh, I've hung around with druggies. I'm a dangerous person now.* Please."

"She didn't like my reaction either. So next time, she drugged me. Just enough morphine to dull my senses but keep me awake. And she made me watch as she... She did what she did."

The man screamed, but there had been a rag in his mouth, soaked in red as he shuddered and kicked. And then the kicking stopped.

"She made me watch one more, and also forced me to help her handle one of the bodies. She was desperate for me to be like her. That's what she kept saying. So one night, I robbed her and I ran."

"And then became a cliched junkie. You were weak."

"I wanted the memories to stop!" I yell.

"How are we the same?" Lorna mutters, almost as though to herself. "Identical, but look at the state of you."

*"She's* the one who told me where you were. I knew she had the contacts, so I reached out. She was happy to tell me."

"Are you sure you don't want one?" Lorna asks, taking down a mug and a glass jar of teabags.

"I told her my plan. That we'd switch places, and eventually one of *them* would catch up to you. I told her that, when they did, they'd probably kill you. At the very least, they'd hurt you badly. Seriously. The sort of injury that requires months of rehab."

"And what did she say?" Lorna asks, still without turning to face me.

"That if they could do that to you, you were no daughter of hers."

"Interesting," Lorna says, still infuriatingly passive.

"Why are you warning me? If you don't care about anything, then why bother?"

"Elizabeth told me about your childhood," Lorna says. "It was easy, apparently. You don't even remember your dad dying."

"I remember *Mum* dying."

"But overall, it was a relatively easy life. You had the regular problems. The nerves about boys. Wondering if you were going to pass the test. That sort of thing."

"To most people, those aren't small problems. Not at that age."

"Like I said – easy, regular. I don't think you're a bad person. Malcolm is. He deserves it. But *you're* not bad. You're just an idiot. So leave, Sadie. Disappear. Find somewhere to raise your baby. Make the baby normal. Turn it into a child who never sees a drop of blood unless they scrape their knee. A child who never has to worry about anything except for tests and boys and bullshit."

"It's almost like you care."

She turns to me, holding her mug of black tea, staring through the steam. "Maybe a little. It's strange. I don't know you, and I've got every reason to hate you. But blood must be thick, because when I think of something bad happening to you, it doesn't feel good. It feels like losing a piece of myself."

"Is this more acting?"

"Believe me or not, it's the truth. But if you're here when something happens…"

"So she *is* going after Malcolm."

"I won't be held responsible," she says, ignoring me.

She leaves the room, and my mind ticks as my heart pounds in my chest. She's just as bad as Mum. I've got to find a woman: have to provide photographs.

I go upstairs, hiding in the bedroom for a while, knowing that the neighbours will get suspicious if they see us together. But from afar, especially with Lorna's hair dyed and hood pulled up, surely they'd be fooled.

But why does it matter, if they're going to kill Malcolm? Am I really willing to die to protect this life? No – the drugs, the sale, then run. Stick to the plan. But either way, I'll need photos, just to keep Malcolm sweet.

---

Later, when Malcolm is snoring next to me, I leave the house and creep down the street. In the dead of night, the sky clear and stars gleaming down, I find the closest telephone box and slot in some change.

When George answers, music pumps in the background. He's using his amped-up voice. He's been on the potions, clearly, elixired up to his eyeballs.

"Yeah? What?"

"It's me."

"Sadie – good. I was trying to ring you."

"I've got the stuff. How soon can you meet?"

"That's what I wanted to tell you... as soon as possible. I'm already in Bristol."

## 55

## LORNA

I hear the crying before I see it.

June, Finn's daughter, is in the arms of a police officer. The woman cradles her gently, talking to the child, as two uniformed policemen escort Finn out of the building, toward the car.

I stay back, staring in awe, listening to my natural aversion for police. Even if their business has nothing to do with me, I always hear Dad's voice, a stern warning to stay clear of them. And now, with all the crime I've been involved with lately, the warning is even louder.

But the crying is the *loudest*, June with her head thrown back, screeching into the sky. Finn is saying something to her, but then one of the policemen shoves his arm gruffly, and Finn bows his head.

My skin crawls as I look at him in his vest, his tattooed arms, the insane attraction I felt towards this pervert. The policewoman carries June to another car, talking to her all the while, with another woman walking at her side in a pencil skirt and suit jacket. They climb into the back of an unmarked vehicle and then they, too, drive away from the building.

Elizabeth watches me from the top window, giving me déjà vu from the last time she did that. When I thought Finn's flat was hers.

I remember what Sadie said, about Elizabeth knowing I was walking blindfolded to my death. She could've warned me easily, but it's like she said, a test. To see if I'm worthy of being her partner-in-death.

But she should have warned me, really. If we dig a pit big enough to fit my husband, I'm sure a skinny, sinewy older lady will fit too.

As I walk up the stairs to her flat, I think about the googling I did on the bus. Elizabeth has published dozens of long-form pieces about the urban underworld, drug dealers, traffickers, people like that, all over England. Now, it seems, she's retired: nothing new for the past two years.

Her work is impressive, and she's right, it gives her the perfect excuse to move around.

"What happened with Finn?" I ask, when she pulls the door open.

"Poor chap." Elizabeth grins, proving that her previous incarnation was a complete act. "It seems somebody had been compiling evidence of his hobby for a couple of months. This somebody was deciding whether or not to send it to the police..."

"Or to take matters into her own hands."

She beams, convinced I'm going along with her, that I'm just as unhinged as she is. And maybe I am; there's no question that Finn deserves to be *under* the prison, let alone in it, after what he did.

"Why do people always turn out to be shitty?" I ask. "I think Sadie might be the only good person I've met since I moved to Weston. Meet a kind elderly lady – she's a serial killer. A handsome man doing his best by his kid – a paedo. The world's a depressing place sometimes."

"Don't be so morbid," Elizabeth says, leading me into her

living room. "We've got plenty to be happy about. Finn's out of the way. The police haven't discovered our little friend in the countryside. We're free to do the right thing, to kill the woman killer."

I could ask her why she didn't warn me. But she'd think I was weak for caring, for *noticing*, even. Plus, it would alert her to the fact I'm not completely okay with this. And that I've recently spoken with Sadie.

The extra risk, the threat to my new life. The fact she was *happy* for those sick bastards to kill me unless I could defend myself. She knew I could, or at least knew I was capable of violence.

But does that make it right? Not in my book. It also means I can't trust her; I'll have to be careful letting in any of these annoying, intrusive feelings of warmth.

"You are ready, aren't you?" she asks. "To kill your husband?"

I offer what I hope is a convincing smile. "Of course I am."

I *should* be. After all he's done to me, after all he's done to others.

But sometimes, when I think of Malcolm, I see the man he was in the beginning, taking pity on the scared, shivering girl after I tried to scam him, laying his hand upon mine. *"Whatever's happening, love, we can make it stop."* And we did. Together.

## 56

## SADIE

It feels wrong taking photos of strangers in public, but at least the woman across the street can't see me. I'm sitting outside the café, my mobile wedged into my paperback, using *burst mode* to capture the woman as she wipes down the table across the street.

She works in another café, young with curls of brown hair and a freckly face. It's schooltime, so I have to assume she's over sixteen. But maybe she's in college, and she's working around her classes. She could be as young as seventeen. It doesn't matter. I'm not going to let anything happen to her.

Just the photos, and I can spin Malcolm a story about her, inventing some mannerisms or personality traits that will have his twisted mind sparking.

I always feel like I can smell George before I see him. I put the book down, pocket my phone, turn and see him swaggering down the street. He's got one hand on the left pocket of his grey tracksuit, and he swings the other almost violently. Tall, muscular, on steroids and stimulants, he almost crushes the seat next to mine when he drops into it.

"All right, Sade."

"You couldn't look like more of a dealer if you tried."

He grins, running a hand through his slick black hair. "If the shoe fits... You got it?"

I glance at a couple walking by across the street. To them, George must seem like a different animal to me. That's a sign of how far I've come, then, with Lorna's clothes and the armour of her life. "It's nearby," I tell him honestly.

"Yeah, so is the cash."

"No – leave the cash here. Then I'll tell you where the package is."

"Are you stupid? After the shit you pulled? I *still* haven't heard from Jonesy, by the way."

We sit on the outskirts of Bristol, a small street, not many people walking by. But there are some on the street, plus the man in the café behind me, and the girl from the photo in the café. I don't have to be afraid of George.

"I haven't heard from him. Listen, George, I swear, the stuff is nearby. I've hidden it. I can draw you a bloody map if you want."

He rests his forearms on the table, causing it to tilt his way. His tattooed forearms seem absurdly big as he clenches his fists. "I can't trust you."

"Well, I don't feel like being hit. Or kidnapped. Or anything else."

"I've got no interest in you. Another slag claiming she's pregnant with my kid? The fuck do I care? But I'm not going to let you rob me. And anyway, I'll need to test the shit. This place you hid it – it quiet?"

I nod. "It should be fine."

"How's the stuff?"

"I obviously haven't tried it."

"What – even a little?"

"I'm pregnant. What's wrong with you?"

How different he seems now, without the drugs draping him in so many projections, none of which were ever real. It's like blood dripping down my vision, being high, except I want to bleed, and everything becomes red, sweet and welcoming and sunset more than scar.

He laughs, takes out his tobacco and starts rolling a cigarette. "Be fair. You know I'm going to need to make sure it's all right before I give you the money. So here's what we're going to do. Take a short walk, have a little sniffle, then we can mosey on our separate ways."

Just then, the employee across the street looks up, the girl I was taking photos of. She gives me the most precious look, a tight frown with her eyes flitting to George, as if she's asking me, *Are you okay?*

What if I show Malcolm this random photo and he takes a liking to her, becomes obsessed enough to kill? I need the money.

I lead George to the bin, reach under the lid where I've taped it, when he pushes a blade against my hip. Even as I start panic breathing, I'm silently screaming at myself. I'm an idiot.

"Grab that package. Don't drop it." With his other hand, George clutches my hip, twisting me around. "Walk, Sade. I'm not going to hurt you. But we're going for a drive."

That's his car across the street, the boy-racer-wannabe vehicle with the stupid flame decals on the side. *I'm not going to hurt you.* Yeah, tell that to the knife pushing firmer and deeper against my back as he manhandles me toward the car.

# A SINGLE GENUINE MOMENT

You always blame external circumstances when something bad happens to you.

Somebody else should've judged what mood you were in, adjusted their behaviour accordingly. There was something wrong with the equipment. You were tired. You were hungry. It's not your fault, whatever it is, always something else.

It's one of the saddest traits in a person. Some go their entire lives without a single genuine moment of self-reflection, without ever stopping to ask... What could *I* have done differently? How could *I* have planned this better?

That's why we're barely the same species, you twisted, Stockholm Syndrome freak. You think control lies outside of yourself. You think the world is out to get you. It's weak, giving up your agency so easily.

Me, I *know* who's in control. I know I've got to do whatever it takes to get the results I want because, ultimately, I'm in charge. I'm the boss and the manager and the employee of my destiny.

I sometimes wonder if, deep down, you know you're far more responsible for your failures than you let the world convince you. Or you convince yourself.

You know it wasn't the wrong day for it. You know it wasn't that you were distracted. You know it has nothing to do with anybody else. It's you, all you, and running from that, hiding from it, denying it, burying it... It turns you into a coward. It makes you even weaker than you already are.

Maybe it's because you know, if you tried to take control, you wouldn't be good enough. You'd fail, just like you do now, only you'd have nobody else to blame.

# 57

## LORNA

lizabeth drives me out into the countryside, taking a different route from last time. It's light now, the sun washing the surrounding hills, the greens seeming starker and cleaner. She simply told me we're going for a drive, with a suggestive look in her eyes... if I argued, after all, she still has that dashcam footage.

"Are you ready to tell me where we're going yet?" I say.

She smiles thinly. "Why would you want to ruin the surprise?"

I don't bother with a response. It would force her to make the dashcam threat explicit. But we're supposed to be past that, a loving mother and daughter. Maybe that's why I take out my phone, thinking of parenthood. Why I look at the photo.

"Who's that?" Elizabeth asks, nodding to the photo of Rachael and Riley on the phone, taken from afar about three months ago.

"The woman Malcolm is having an affair with. Or was. I'm not sure if he still is. They have a son together."

I smile at the memory, Malcolm always on edge during her birth month. He called Rachael his colleague, never explicitly stating what she was, but we both knew it. And on the night

Rachael gave birth, Malcolm was the one to drive her to the hospital.

To help his *colleague*. But I saw that goodness in him, a hint of it, a glint, nothing much. He cares about the boy in his own way.

I don't tell Elizabeth my reason for taking the photo; Rachael was going to be the next woman, the next victim of the box. Malcolm had dropped countless hints about it, like a regular man might hint at a coveted Christmas present.

"She's not a good mother," I say. "She leaves him often, even when she doesn't have to. She doesn't even seem to love him. If I had a child… I'd always love them. I'd never abandon them."

"I'm sure Rachael has her reasons," Elizabeth replies. "Her own demons. Women are far smarter than men. We sense when something's off, even if we don't know the reason."

"He would be better off with me," I say.

Elizabeth scowls. "What?"

I go on. "You can't pretend that a child *has* to remain with the birth mother, not after what you did."

"Was that your plan?" Elizabeth asks. "To kill Rachael and steal her son, raise him as your own?"

I stare out the window, at the far too beautiful countryside, the annoyingly bright sun. That thought had crossed my mind, I won't lie – well, to myself. I'll lie to Elizabeth as much as she makes me.

"Malcolm kills women. We don't. We kill the men who hurt women. I understand you had to do some things in your old life. I've met Malcolm. He's terrifying, when he wants to be. I get it, Lorna. But you'd never choose that for yourself, would you?"

I turn to her, look at her steadily as she drives, her jaw tensed, jutting out of her old skin.

"My mum knew what was happening with my dad," I say. "She caught him, on several occasions, doing what he did. To my young body. In various ways. But she always pretended not to know. Once, at a party, she got drunk and asked why I was always behaving like a slut around my dad. My own mother said that to me."

"I'm so sorry, Lorna."

"But she's alive. In Scotland. Her mind isn't. That died a few years ago. But her body keeps going."

"You killed the man, not the woman. That's good."

Good or not, it doesn't change the truth. I'm willing to kill anybody. Even you, Elizabeth.

So many pieces of me have died along the way – Dad's attention, Mum's blindness, the rush and then the seeping away of Malcolm's love, the killings, the stillbirth smashed against the wall as if it never held any significance...

That man: I hate him, but he's all I know. My thoughts spin and hurt.

Elizabeth pulls off the road onto a bumpy track, and then turns again down a small lane. She climbs out of the car, walking down between the tall trees. The path isn't a *path* as such, more a cleared-away section of undergrowth, the grass and weeds already creeping back.

"Where are we?" I ask. "And please – no more *surprise* talk."

Elizabeth tucks her thumbs into her denim dungarees, smiling at me, truly beautiful with her hair tied up, her features sharp. I wonder if I'll look as dignified at her age.

"A private allotment. I have some interesting ideas about the soil."

# 58

## SADIE

**M**y hands are tight on the steering wheel, eyes flitting every so often to the satnav. George sits in the passenger seat, the knife casually pressed into my side, following me even if I squirm away, maintaining the same pressure.

"Where are we going?" I ask, as we drive out of Bristol, heading down the motorway, deeper into Somerset.

"Just keep driving."

"Take the drugs *and* the money. I don't care."

He grins, dipping his finger into the bag with his free hand, smearing it over his teeth, all while I drive eighty miles per hour and struggle to keep my hands steady.

I *hate* myself. Lorna was right. I'm naïve. I'm finally seeing myself for what I am, a middle-class woman who thinks, because she's had a few years of hell in the rough side of life, she really understands it. But I fell for him, *again*. I thought I was smarter.

Even sober, he can cast his spell on me. Maybe the effect is less, but it must still be there, the ringleader who got them all riled up, who tricked my splintered, drugged mind into thinking I was being cool, that I was *involved*, until things turned nasty.

And by then, it was too late. They weren't men anymore. Just animals with glazed-over eyes.

"It's good stuff, too," he says, laughing. "You know, word on the street is there's a bloke looking for a bag just this size. The mule had a house party, and it disappeared. Too many people to track down. Not like there was a guest list. So you're right. This shit *is* mine. Everybody assumes it's already lost."

"So then where are we going?" I whisper, taking the exit that leads toward Devon.

"For a little drive, that's all. A friend of mine is pretty keen to say hello."

"What friend?"

He closes the bag, then sniffles several times. "Somebody who knows all your secrets. This is bigger than me and you and a few grand now. It seems you've landed on your feet. I've got photos of you and the old bastard, and *you* in his house..."

"How?" I demand. He's clearly talking about Malcolm.

"You'll start singing soon enough. It's a long game, you see. You're going to work with us to fleece that old wanker for all he's worth. But first, I need to remind you of who I am. We agreed I'd have some time with you before business. There's even a mattress, if things get really out of hand."

I close my legs tightly, shivering, as the satnav takes me away from the motorway, into the land of green fields and one-lane roads. The surroundings are too peaceful, giving me time to wonder who this *friend* is. I've got an idea, but I can't believe it. Can't accept it, at least. Even after everything, I'm here, I'm breathing.

"What's this joker doing?" George grunts, as a car begins to speed behind us, coming right up on the rear of our vehicle. "Go faster, Sade. Fucking idiot."

I do as he says, but the car keeps coming, and then I see the driver. My heart leaps, joy expanding, and I warn myself to stop, to kill it, to *never* feel that way at the sight of this man.

Malcolm, grimacing, leaning forward and waving his hand at me to pull over.

"I'll have to move to the side," I say. "This is too dangerous."

George spins in his seat, shouting. *"Watch where you're bloody going, you..."* He trails off. He looks at me, looks at the man. Knows why he's here: to save me.

The car spins as I jump for the knife. I have to. George is trying to stab me.

# 59

## LORNA

The so-called allotment is really just a few flowerbeds and some weeds, the grass overgrown between the small stone steps.

"I've only had it a couple of weeks," she says. "I haven't been up here much, but I will. You'll see. If I choose to stay in this little corner of England, this will be an oasis."

She's oddly attractive as she walks ahead, smiling at me like a proud kid showing off a project. She walks to the edge of a pit.

From my spot behind her, it looks small.

Then I join her at the edge. I'm looking down into a grave, mud stacked on the other side, the rectangle walls impressively flat, the hole deeper than I'd imagined she was capable of.

"How long did this take?" I ask.

"All day. Eight hours, perhaps more. I was dead by the end of it. Well – not as dead as the thing we're going to put inside, of course."

"Thank God it didn't rain," I tell her. "This would've filled up."

She grins. "Now we get to fill it with something else."

She thinks she's being so slick, so *cool*.

"Yeah – Malcolm. You drove me all the way out here for *that?*"

"It's not Malcolm," Elizabeth says, fiddling with her hair. "And *your* mood isn't helping things. I could've told you about the hole. No, you're here because somebody is coming to meet us. I'm going to do something I should've done a long time ago."

She puts her hands on her hips, looking down at the hole with the air of a workman studying a job well done.

"Who?" I ask.

She taps her nose. "That would be telling. Don't spoil the fun."

## 60

## SADIE

The car slows and comes to a bumpy stop as I desperately claw onto George's wrist. But now George pushes against me, far stronger than he has any right to be with the way he treats his body. I lean against the car door, gasping as I struggle to control his hand, the knife hissing past my face as he moves in jerky motions, suddenly, violently.

A single slash could end my life. Or blind me. Bleed me out.

"*Stop! Stop!*" I scream.

Then, behind him, I see Malcolm. He's got that furious look on his face, the one that melted his little brother at dinner. Weirdly, he looks somehow attractive, the thought flashing across my mind in the wildness of the fight.

Not handsome. Not pretty. Not *good*, even, but attractive in his fury. He yanks the door open, then leans down and grabs George's ankles. He pulls on him sharply, dragging him out of the car, George slashing the side of the driver's seat and tearing down it with the blade. The sound, *scrrrrr*, is impossibly loud.

Then Malcolm's on him, his hands moving in sudden flashes of a fight, his fists catching the sunlight as he hits George once, hard, right on the end of his nose. I hear a *crunch* noise and George yells as his nose breaks.

I climb from the car, staring down as Malcolm stands, his chest heaving, spit covering his chin, eyes wide and insane. He glares at George, who's moaning and touching his face. "Don't try anything." He looks at me. "I told you, we'd do this together."

George raises his hand weakly. Malcolm bends down and picks up the knife. George grunts, his senses seeming to clear from the blow. Suddenly, he attempts to stand. Malcolm swings his foot into a vicious kick, landing on George's belly. He gasps and collapses, hands covering his middle.

"Rat," Malcolm growls. "Where's the cash, Lorna?" He spins, powerfully throwing the knife into the adjacent field.

My instincts freeze when he uses that name. George doesn't know anything about the switch. From his place on the ground, George opens his mouth, blood streaming from his nose and down on his face. He glances at Malcolm, holding the knife, then sits up, his hands on his belly.

"In the car," I say, struggling to breathe.

"Get it. Leave the coke. Last thing we need is a war with some druggie fucks. You hear that?" Malcolm raises his voice as he kicks George again. "We're leaving your shit. Whatever you were planning, it ends here. You're lucky I don't kill you."

I'm wondering why he doesn't. But of course, he only kills women. That's what excites him. Or maybe it's just practical, like he said. Avoiding a war. I get the cash from the car, returning as George struggles to a sitting position.

"The fuck's he calling you Lorna for, Sadie?"

I laugh, ensuring the laugh has a tinge of Scottish accent, like I'm that girl in Mum's bedroom again, capable of playing any role, of becoming any character she wished for.

"What new game is this?"

*Gaaeemmmm.* Fuck, Malcolm is narrowing his eyes at me. I can't remember if I was using the Scottish accent when I was screaming at George about the knife. Why would I be? It was probably my regular accent.

Now, as Malcolm watches me, I'm sure he's combing over the past few days, every minor interaction, wondering... But surely, it's like I said to Lorna in the beginning. This is so ridiculous, so insane, nobody would ever assume that *twins* would be the explanation.

"He's trying to trick us," I go on.

"What did you call her?" Malcolm says, walking over to the man, fists clenched.

Malcolm walks in front of me, and I stare around him at George. I clasp and raise my hands pathetically, in a begging gesture. I make my eyes wide, how he used to like them when I was high and disconnected and he was doing what he wanted.

Everything I aim at him screams, *Please, please!* He's got no reason to, but then he gives a subtle nod, the tiniest nod, one most people wouldn't notice. But I was attuned to this man for a long time. I get it – leave the cash. So I motion with the bag, and he grins up at Malcolm. It all happens so fast.

"I was calling her a slutty, mate, because that's what she is." As he talks, I creep backward, then drop the bag near the wheel of the car. George goes on. "A real stupid gullible suburban bi—"

He doesn't get any further. Malcolm punches him in the face again. George yelps and collapses onto the ground. He's badly beaten up, but I've seen far, far worse than that in my old life. This is a borderline civilised beating, a couple of punches, a kick.

Then, as Malcolm walks back toward me, trembling all over, George sits up and gives me a crooked smile. Almost like one criminal to another, saying, *Whatever scam you're running, good job.* But the smile drops when I pick up the cash, shrugging as he struggles to stand. He shouts after us, wasting the chance he has. He could reveal who I am. But he just swears, threatens. It's classic George.

"Get in the bloody car," Malcolm snaps at me, throwing the

door open. He drops into the driver's seat, then grabs the bag of cash and opens it roughly, grunts, nods, and shoves it into the footwell. "What were you thinking?" he roars, slamming his hand against the steering wheel. "Going alone? While pregnant? Why, Lorna?"

He's calling me Lorna. He's showing no sign of believing what George said – and he amended it, *slutty, Sadie*. From an injured man, they sound similar enough, don't they?

"I thought it would be better if only one of us was involved," I whisper, not having to try hard to summon the tears. "That way, if I was caught, at least you'd be free to r-r-r-*raise*..."

I scream on the last word, and then the tears come, not fake, just not genuine to this moment exactly. It's all the fear stacked up from George, the knife, the memories, the pain. He's walking toward the car now, yelling at us, face bright red from his busted nose.

"Lucky we don't run him over," Malcolm grunts, reversing. "Don't worry. I'm not going to hurt you. Or the baby. But from now on, we're a team, all right?"

"Yes, definitely. I'm sorry. Yeah."

He spins the car around. "Then let's get out of here."

In the rear-view, George screams and waves his hands like a vision from a horror film.

"Did you follow me?" I ask.

When Malcolm laughs, there's something almost kind about it, indulgent but not in a patronising way.

"Yeah, and it was a nightmare, like a scene out of a spy novel. Especially on the motorway. But I wasn't going to let anything happen to you. It all looked good until you got into the car."

"Thank you." I lay my hand on his arm, not sure if I'm faking this part. "Really."

"I may not be perfect, but I'll always protect you."

# 61

## LORNA

"Ah, finally."

Elizabeth stands from the foldout chair. We've been sitting here for ages, but we haven't bonded like one might imagine. We talked mostly about different kinds of fertilisers, Elizabeth speaking with passion, as though she's not my mother, as though there isn't a whole secret life inside of her. But there's one in me too, and I don't feel like sharing.

She walks to the gate at the sound of the car, pulling it open, then sticks her hands on her hips and frowns. A boy-racer-type car pulls up, and a man with a bloody face steps out. His nose is a mess, and I walk closer, wondering if this is the person we're waiting for. His attack was recent, clearly.

He yells when he sees me, raising his hands. "Fucking *bitch*."

When he rushes at me, I've got no choice but to spin and dart away. I've been hit by the male species enough times to know that head-on is rarely the best approach.

A glance over my shoulder shows me he's chasing me across the allotment, tramping through the long grass, and Elizabeth is doing *nothing* to help. She rests her hand on the gate, watching impassively.

Another test. Fuck you, *Mum*.

Suddenly, I dart one way, causing the man to slip slightly. Then I grab a trowel, the closest weapon I can find, sitting next to an uncared-for flowerbed. I hit him across the face, twice, until he screams and falls back.

"Bitch," he groans.

"Why did you do that?" I shout.

The man blinks. "I'm losing it. I'm done. What's happening? Edie – you hear me?"

Elizabeth wanders over. "I'm here. Where is she? You said you'd bring her."

He blinks again, staring up at me, then his eyes refocus. "Fuck me. No. No goddamn way. That's too much. Don't make me laugh. Ah, it hurts." But he can't stop himself, exploding into laughter as the dried blood cracks on his face and droplets weep.

"Care to explain, *Edie?*"

Elizabeth waves her hand. "A fake name, nothing special."

"Yeah, obviously. But who is this bastard, and why was he trying to kill me?" Elizabeth looks at me like I'm stupid, then I realise I am. "He knows Sadie."

"Yes, he does." Elizabeth kneels, gesturing at me for the trowel. When I hand it over, she whacks him on the side of the face, not overly hard, but enough to make a bony noise.

"What are you doing?" she hisses, as the man groans. "Look, Lorna. *Look.*"

"It's disgusting."

"You've *done* worse."

"But not like this. Not when I'm cold."

"Oh, Lord. Shall I wait for you to do some stretching?"

"Reality isn't…"

"What?" she demands.

"Oh, fuck off!" I shout, stomping to the other side of the allotment. "I don't care who he is. Or what you've got planned."

"Yes, you do. This here is George, a rather impressive man in

228

his contained world. He's the ringleader who initiated the gang rape of Sadie. That's why I tricked and lied to the gullible goon; he was going to bring her here, and she was going to *watch*. She was going to see how good it is, what I do, how righteous."

As her voice takes on an almost religious tenor, George continues to whine, legs kicking.

"Why isn't he fighting back?"

She giggles, sounding far younger than she is. "Tell her, Georgie."

She's doing it ironically, the *It* impression, mimicking the clown's voice. She rolls her eyes at me as if we're both in on the joke, laughing at the mangled man on the floor.

"Just some videos and that," he says through a blood-filled mouth, voice slurring. Any more violence and he won't be able to speak.

"Yes, some videos of George doing some very naughty things. He filmed them himself. Sadie's in them, Lorna."

She stands, wincing when her bones crack, and takes a step back.

I wander closer, as the sun shines down and nature makes its noises around us.

A siren passes by in the distance. George laughs gruffly as he sits up, his breath wheezy, his nose battered and cheek bruised. But he's stopped bleeding now. He's definitely on something, a stimulant driving him through the pain. "We're over here, officer. Sorry, all right? Bloody twin? Fuck me. Listen, Edie, or whatever your name is, I'll just be on my way, all right?"

*"All right, all right,"* Elizabeth says, mimicking his whiny voice as she waggles her eyebrows at me.

This is like what Malcolm takes from the games, the sick run-up, the excitement, the hunger in his eyes. It's the same as Elizabeth, but then, what am I – am I better?

"What did you do to Sadie in the video?" I say, moving closer to him.

"Nothing," he grunts, standing up. He's acting tough, but he's shaking. "What happened to your face?"

"Sadie's new man."

Malcolm.

"You let that fat pig beat you to a pulp?" Elizabeth laughs, throwing her head back, clapping hands in a civilised way like we're at a party. "Christ, I thought you were supposed to be some street tough nut, uncrackable, you. Aye, George?"

He bristles, shaking his head. "Got me from behind."

"And yet it's your face that's a mess."

Elizabeth shouldn't laugh at Malcolm. He's not bloody laughable.

"What happened in the video?" I say, stepping closer, and staring George right in the eye.

"Nothing."

"It's quite simple. George and Jonesy and a few of the others turned Sadie into a rag doll."

*Stop*, I say, but I can't shape the words. My mind is flashing with the muted intimacy Malcolm and I shared. Sometimes, rarely, there was pleasure, near love, but always tinged with what we had done. Other times, it was duty.

But there are times before when I was so small I can hardly believe it, that a thing that tiny and simple can exist, and things were done, and I swallowed it down and never thought about it, but sometimes reality weeps like my heart is bleeding for my sister, my twin I never knew, don't want to know, but it's like a part of me – what he did to her – it died in the same—

And now Elizabeth is yelling, laughing, and there's a judder going up my arm. Another one, like a hammer strike at the base of my palm. I fall back with the impact.

My vision is blurred with tears and there's snot all over my upper lip.

"He did it, Lorna," Elizabeth says from behind me. "He knew

Sadie couldn't consent. And when she passed out, *he* was the one who egged the others—"

Silence, nothing, hardly any sensation. It's like I've dropped into the bottom of a deep well. Elizabeth's voice is the only real thing. As sick as it is, it's the only time I've felt a mother-daughter bond in my life, when her voice joins me in this lonely place.

"He's a monster. He showed me the videos himself. And he's an idiot, believed I was some big criminal. That's it. Keep going. Good girl."

A haze over everything, but my body must be responding to my mother's instructions. I can feel faint shudders now, and I open my eyes, hear my own yelling, a guttural throaty thing, hardly any noise.

I'm too tired to yell. I've mangled his face with the trowel. There's nothing human left. I crawl away, gasping, then vomit all over the grass.

Elizabeth kneels next to me, softly placing her hand on my shoulder. "I'm so proud of you. Come on, chin up. Go get a drink. I've got some water in the car. I'll take care of this mess."

I stumble away, crawling through the grass, somehow drag myself to my feet. But then I make a mistake – glancing over there. No, it's bad. What I did. *How* did I do that?

"Be a dear, Lorna. When you're in the car, grab the satnav. It was foolish to use it, really."

"They can upload to the Cloud," I say, glad to have something else to focus on.

"Am I some rookie reporter sucking dick to get the inside scoop about the local pub ownership scandal, Lorna?" she yells.

I ignore her, grabbing the satnav. It's on airplane mode.

"And who says the elderly can't use technology?"

The banter's all well and good until I return to her. There's too much messiness in his face.

"How are you this squeamish?"

"I'm not," I say, taking a breath. "It's just – sometimes, it's like I'm not there."

"Yeah," Elizabeth says, frowning down at George's body. "That's an old, old story, sweetheart. Monster abuses angel. Angel learns how to set its wings on fire so it doesn't have to feel it. And then that burning won't stop. Do you understand me?" She looks at me intensely, like a cult member.

"Yeah."

"Really, dear, go sit down. I'll clean all this up."

Without looking, I throw the satnav onto the ground, then stumble to the edge of the allotment.

"Don't you ever wonder where the police are?" I ask.

Elizabeth titters as she pulls a pair of garden gloves on. "They'll get us eventually. They always do."

"I was thinking that earlier."

"But there's no need to make it easy. Georgie and Jonesy – that'll be a drug feud gone wrong. Two dealers missing… it's not like anybody's going to be looking for them. George and his compatriots are lowlifes. Malcolm will be harder to get away with. People will look for a motive."

She eyes me with significance, the sun shining down on her beautiful hair. "We'd be wise to think of a plausible one – that would lead elsewhere. But that would require knowing all his dirty little secrets."

Again with the smile, like we're in this together. My hands are wet with blood, but already, I can feel them matting. It's in my hair. On my face. In my mouth. I can taste the man I killed.

"Did he really do it?" I ask, ignoring her hint.

She wants me to betray Malcolm. Which is what *I* should want, too. "Oh, he did it," Elizabeth says. "And much, much worse. I should've done this long ago: when he first got Sadie hooked on his filth. The world's a better place without him."

I let my head fall back on the wooden fencing surrounding the allotment, closing my eyes. "All right, good."

# FINALLY

People are wrong about the Bible. That's self-evident, you might say, but I'm talking about something specific, and I don't necessarily agree it *is* self-evident. Just because you've always seen yourself as above mere mortals, it doesn't mean you are.

You're a person, as unlikely as that seems.

The commandment not to kill is not as imperative as people think it is; it's not the instruction to never take a life. The translation is off. There are over half a dozen words used in the Old Testament alone: for slaying, rendering lifeless, whatever one wishes to call it.

You mustn't slaughter a person for no reason. But if they are a killer, then you're allowed to kill them. And David killed more than a Goliath. The point is quite clear – there is a justification for killing.

I don't believe there's any defence for what I did to you – as I've willingly stated – but there's more than enough justification for my other life-stealing escapades.

There's plenty of blame to go around.

I'm sure you like to pretend it's difficult. You yourself, perhaps in the final moments, attempt to convince your sick soul the tightening of your grip is involuntary. Or a challenge, your own Goliath to slay. But you're not complicated enough for that.

You're not intelligent. You're an idiot. A fucking moron right down to your bones.

That's why this has to happen. My way. Finally.

## 62

## SADIE

It's been two days since the stuff with George, and in all that time, Malcolm hasn't touched me. He's locked himself in the spare room, coughing and wheezing.

"That little shit gave me the flu," he says through the door, when I bring him his breakfast this morning.

Two days of waiting, of wondering if the police are going to arrive. Or George, returning to take revenge. And the *friend* he was taking me to… who was that? I have an idea, but I don't think Elizabeth would hurt me. Maybe she was playing some game.

If not her – some other druggy lowlife who could appear at any moment. And a husband who's behaving strangely.

"Have you got my food or not?" he says.

"Yes, sorry."

I push the door open with my elbow. He's sitting up in bed, shirtless, with the window wide open, looking down on the immaculate garden. I lay the tray down, and then move as if to kiss him. Not because I want or need the affection. Definitely not from him. But because it's *necessary* for what I'm doing here.

He hid the cash when we got home. A safety deposit box somewhere; it must be. We came home. He left in the car, with the cash, then returned without it. He moves away from me. "You don't want to get it too."

"Maybe I'm willing to take the risk," I say, and, like I have been ever since the George incident, I'm questioning the accent.

It's like I'm constantly watching myself, judging. "And the baby – we need to keep him safe."

"Or her."

"Yes, or her. Please, Lorna."

I turn, walk away, thinking about my failure.

"Make a personal connection with her today," he says.

I almost keep walking, ignoring his orders, but I have to keep doing what Lorna would. Which, as sick as it is, means returning to that café, hoping the same girl is working.

"Get to a position where she'll agree to go for a drive with you," he says. "But be careful about being too easily identified. You might even want to think about changing your accent."

I look at him, expecting an arched eyebrow, some *got you* sign, but he's not even looking at me. Am I being paranoid?

"Yeah, I'll do that," I say, full Scot.

Definitely *not* an Englishwoman barely holding on, wondering with every single word if she sounds like a bad actor or, worse, an accidental racist.

---

Malcolm is ill for three more days, giving me no way to search for the cash or hatch an escape plan. I'm his servant day and night. He shoots me texts when he wants something instead of ringing a bell, but it's basically the same. It's a sad thing, isn't it, the fact I don't disobey once? I saw what he did to George.

I go to the café at ten in the morning, and sit in the window seat. Being in a café gives me flashbacks to George. But this has nothing to do with him. I open Lorna's – my – laptop, and start pretend-typing. But somewhere along the way, I get into it, beginning to *really* type. Once upon a time, I loved books, and would have loved to be a writer.

I don't write about my life, just weird little poems, rubbish really. But I notice the young woman looking over as she wipes down a table. Up this close, her cheeks are rosy, like her youth is bursting out of her. And an ugly part of me knows that's what Malcolm seeks, a vampire feasting on her infancy.

"I'm sorry," she says, looking away.

"You don't have to apologise, Charlotte," I say, reading her name tag.

"Are you a poet?"

"I'm just messing around, really," I say.

"I'm studying English."

Oh, fate, you cruel bitch. I've got something in common with the girl I'm stalking. I've been careful with my seat, sitting where the camera isn't facing, but they'll still have me coming in.

"At university?" Please.

"At college. A level. I'm in my second year. I love it – really. I want to be a writer." She bubbles up with conversation, and I almost cry at how young she seems.

"Sorry. You just don't see people writing poems very often."

"Stop saying sorry," I snap.

I must come across as too aggressive. She bows her head, moves on to the next table. A while later, my mobile rings. "Any progress?" His voice is so aggressive, so different since the so-called flu scare. The stuff with George. The doubt. The hints.

Or maybe I'm just driving myself mad. I should've hidden the cash before he had a chance to move it. "We've talked."

"Tell me her name, then."

"Charlotte," I say, feeling sick.

"Right. Anything else? What have you been *doing*?"

"I was... pretending to write poetry."

He laughs savagely. "Jesus."

"And she told me she studies English at college."

"College? So she's what – seventeen, eighteen?"

I swallow, almost experiencing pain.

"Yeah."

"Then listen close. You're going to tell pretty little Charlotte that you run a poetry class. You won't give her your phone number. You can meet there one evening and walk together – it's just around the corner. Do you understand?"

"Malcolm..."

"This is what's happening. Or I'll beat your belly so badly the next time I see you, dear wife, there won't be anything left. Am I making myself clear?"

"Yes," I say, as genuine terror cuts through me.

When Charlotte circles back around, I try to stop myself from doing it. It's complete cowardice; that's the excuse I give to myself. It has nothing to do with how Malcolm flew to my rescue, saved me. There aren't – can't be – warm feelings here.

"A club?" Charlotte says, raising her eyebrows. "And I could come?"

I shrug. No big deal. Hating myself. "If you like. It's just around the corner. We could meet here and walk together?"

She's far too naïve. It's *me*, a mirror, before my mum died, before my other mum arrived.

"Oh, yeah, that'd be great. Are you sure? When is it?"

"Um – Wednesday."

The *um* was a mistake. At the least the accent was decent.

That gives me three days to think of how to save her life.

"I don't even know your name," Charlotte says.

For a second, I think this might be reasonable suspicion, but it's not. It's anxiety; I read it in her face, the anxiety of getting too far into our relationship without asking, and then it becomes awkward. It's a pedestrian pointless response. Why won't she just *run*?

"I'm Lorna. So, you'd like to come?"

"Yes, only if you're sure."

Not even a little bit, Charlotte.

# 63

## LORNA

It's somehow exhilarating, following Malcolm through the shopping centre. He walks idly in and out of shops, sometimes with a small purchase – a book, a sausage roll – but more often without.

Elizabeth is at my side, both of us in sunglasses, Covid-style masks, though the pandemic is past us now. I don't even like thinking about it, honestly, being locked up with *him*. We trail him through the centre and then down the busy Bristol street into a large park.

It would've been different before, maybe, when we were younger, cared enough to pretend. Could we ever get back there? No – focus. I'm wearing baggy clothes too, *and* I'm walking with a cane.

"Do you think he's looking for his next victim?" Elizabeth asks as we sit on one side of the park, Malcolm on the other, watching people, dog walkers and mothers with children and an elderly couple holding hands.

It's a large park; I can't make out his expression. "I doubt it."

"Really – why?"

"He doesn't do the initial part. The – stalking." A hitch in my voice. I don't like speaking about this.

"You did that part." I can feel her looking at me. "Because you had no choice."

"It still doesn't make it all right. There's no forgiveness for it." I can't let my mind stray to the women.

"How many?" Elizabeth asks, as though wanting to force me.

Counting them in my mind takes a moment. Not because the number is astronomical – though, one is too many – but because each one comes with a flare of violent memory. With the stench of blood and piss and screaming, and wishing for it all to end, *me* wishing that. "Four," I tell her.

"You're like a madam in a brothel for necrophiliacs."

"You're so witty, *Mum*."

She laughs throatily when I call her that, bringing my mind back to the allotment, the murder, and how casually she filled in the hole. Toward the end, I stood nearby, watching this old lady work, admiring the sinewy power of her body. "What *is* he doing, then?"

"He's still a human being," I tell her.

Another laugh. "What?"

"I'm just saying, you don't need to invent a whole new way of thinking about him. He might just be enjoying his lunch break. It might have nothing to do with the you-know-what."

"The acquisition, rape, and murder of a young woman, just so we're clear."

I swallow a lump. The past hurts.

Being in the room – experiencing it, fearing it, and then trying to run… and Malcolm, momentarily abandoning his task, beating me so badly all I could do was roll onto my side and watch. If I looked away… I couldn't then, fine, but I can now.

"The fear never goes away," I whisper, staring at the vague figure of Malcolm, his outline more than anything. And for a second, reality wavers and it grows horns. "The reflex of wanting to apologise. Of *knowing* he'll find a way to hurt me for this."

"I understand. It took me decades to let go of what certain people did to me."

What I don't say is something I can barely acknowledge to myself: the hope never goes either. That the good times will become the norm, that we'll leave the pain behind. It's not like the outside world is better, is it? Finn is a monster. My birth mother would've happily let drug dealers kill me. My long-lost sister is a naïve and yet manipulative idiot.

"It won't be long now," Elizabeth says.

"How will you do it?"

"*We.*"

I wait, and she goes on, "You'll lure him outside at night, away from the house, from the alarm. That will be easy if we think of a good excuse. Then I'll inject him with a heavy tranquilliser. We'll arrange it so he's very close to the car. Put him in the boot. Drive him out to the special place."

"You make it sound so easy."

"Killing isn't the hard part," she says. "Getting away with it is. I don't usually do this."

"Multiple people in one spot?"

"These are special circumstances."

"Why?"

She turns, takes off her sunglasses. "Because you're my daughter."

I wish I could believe that motherly devotion was her true motivation, but there's something fake there.

"Anyway, there's no use hanging around. We know where to find him. This is senseless sport more than anything. Once I've got the right vehicle, we'll be ready."

"What's the *right vehicle*?"

"One that came from nowhere and will disappear into nowhere once we're done."

I try to imagine Malcolm trussed up in the boot of a car, or in the back of a van, but the image simply won't fit in my mind.

"Maybe we should keep watching," I say. "He might do something before we make our move, hurt someone... Do we want that on our conscience?"

Toward the end of my sentence, I realise what I'm doing. It's the warble in my voice. It's not that it's *fake* exactly, but I put more emotion into it than I really need to.

My feelings are conflicted, honestly. There's something terrifyingly alluring about seeing Malcolm, which, I think, is the real reason I stayed with him despite all the evil stuff.

That attraction, that pull, which shouldn't exist after all he's done. All I've done. The feeling I got when he held my eighteen-year-old hands and told me, "Nothing will ever hurt you, Lorna, not when I'm here." I'm pathetic. I need to *kill* that part.

"You mean, you can't have that on *your* conscience," Elizabeth says.

I nod, sniffling, *sniffling*, which is a touch over the top. But I can't help myself.

"You wouldn't do anything silly, would you?" she says, narrowing her eyes.

I'm glad I'm still hidden behind my sunglasses and my face mask. It gives me the freedom to analyse her. She's not talking about revealing myself to him, becoming his ally, his wife again.

She means: will I kill him without her?

"I saw how savage you were with our good friend Georgie. I wouldn't want you losing control."

"I won't. And I won't get close, either."

She replaces her sunglasses. "I'm fairly confident in your ability to follow people, dearie, don't worry about that. If anything happens, ring me. And... well, you're steady, aren't you, Lorna?"

"Steady?"

"You understand why we're doing this, you and I. You *see*. I know you had your squeamish moment, but you're like me. What we do, it's the righteous thing, the *good* thing. Don't let your past marriage complicate things."

Insanity, but part of me cringes when she calls it my *past* marriage.

"He's nothing to me," I tell her. "When the time comes, he'll see that."

Then she leans forward. "But really, Lorna, it might be better to just leave."

I shake my head, purposefully not too hard. I don't want to seem overly keen. "I'd like to see what he's up to. If he targets another woman... I want to stop him."

The tilt of Elizabeth's head, my masked face reflected in her glasses, gives me no indication if she believes me. But she must, on some level, because she finally nods. "Very noble of you. Just be careful, okay?"

"I will," I reply.

She leaves, and I continue watching Malcolm with the safety of distance. Eventually, he stands, walks a circuit of the park. He walks right by me and I sit back, holding my breath, waiting for the moment.

But *his* Lorna wouldn't be wearing torn leggings and chunky boots and, anyway, my face is almost completely covered. There's no way he could recognise me.

His hand is twitching, as if he wants to inflict violence. But of course he does. He's holding a paper cup. He drops it as he passes, spilling coffee.

Turns, looks right at me. Our eyes meet. Time does bizarre, torturous things. Or my eyes meet his, and his meet my sunglasses, which suddenly feel pitiful.

My heart pounds hard as I ride the bus back to the flats. I can still smell the coffee, and the panic hasn't left me. I know what's just happened. All of this, collapsing back on itself. All my high-and-mighty ideals. I spoke to him. His voice has a power over me that makes me so, so ashamed.

When I walk up the street to what was *supposed* to be my sanctuary, when this all started, the panic amplifies. My father yelling at me, *Never trust the pigs, good for nothing, sweetie.* Two police officers climb from their car and walk straight at me. There's no mistaking who they're here for.

I remember what Elizabeth and I joked about in the allotment, the police, their absence. Well, here they are.

"Sadie Newington?" the male officer says, sniffling.

On the younger side, bright blue eyes, blond hair beneath his hat. The woman is a couple of inches taller than him, wide shoulders, and she already looks like she hates me. Staring at me like I'm guilty. But I'm a good actress. Complete confusion. "Yes?"

"Would you mind if we had a little chat?" the male officer says.

"Can I ask what this is about?"

"It would be better if we talked inside," the woman says stiffly. Hmm. They've got no right to come into my flat. But also, I *know* it's clean, and I have to present a certain image.

"Of course," I tell her, and then I nearly add, *I've got nothing to hide.*

# 64

## SADIE

"What do you think?" Malcolm says, like a proud craftsman displaying his wares. "Not bad, is it?"

We're standing in a metal shack on the outskirts of a field. There's a mattress on the floor and an oil lamp throws light against the grimy walls, with dusky sunlight seeping through the cracks in the ceiling.

"Not bad," I repeat, staring, hating, thinking of the cash I stupidly let him take.

"Not sound-proofed," he goes on, walking in a circle around the small space. "But out here, I don't think it needs to be. Plus, we can always gag her… in more ways than one."

There's no forgiveness for me: the fact I'm here, hearing *jokes* like this. "Do you like it?" He approaches me quickly, my hands in his, and, pathetically, I'm relieved. He's touching me again. But then he says, "It's not quite as pretty as the other spots, is it?"

Accent, *firm*, not like the car, when I was screaming. His eyes are seemingly innocent, but that could be an act. "It's even more perfect," I say, and then I throw myself at him.

And when I say throw, I mean it. It's up there with the most nauseating things I've had to do in my life. But it's necessary, because I can't tolerate the questions anymore. The endless wondering.

He catches me, kisses me; his mouth tastes of cigarettes. And then we collapse onto the grimy mattress: the spot where Charlotte will be destroyed. I hate myself. Soon, it will be time to run. I need that cash. Where is he hiding it?

He stops the kissing, shoving my face away, pushing my cheek against the mattress. It stinks like damp. "That's it. You'll pretend to be her, won't you? Pretend to be poor little Charlotte?" His eyes are wild.

I've willingly put my baby's life in this man's hands. Maybe I'm slower than I thought, because, as we do it – as I fulfil the role he desires – I can't believe it's taken me so long to understand this.

The first time his brother made a move, or the first time he hit me, the night he took it so far the physical agony is still there…

"What's your name?" Malcolm growls, mid-act.

For a second, I think he knows. He expects me to say *Sadie*. Then I remember.

"Charlotte. Charlotte."

"That's right."

# 65

## LORNA

PC Davis (the angry-looking woman) and PC Keane (the sniffling man) sit across from me, the coffee table between us. I spent a long time brewing their teas, preparing myself for whatever role I'll need to play. They don't look comfortable on the second-hand sofa cushions I bought to replace the burned ones. And luckily, they clearly aren't suspicious of the stains on the tatty material.

Davis stirs sugar into her tea as if she's trying to break the mug, the tap-tap-tap of her spoon louder than it has any right to be. Keane keeps trying to catch my eye, a smile beginning to form on his lips. None of it will work. I'm an innocent woman, confused by their presence; that's all they'll ever see. *Pigs*, Dad grunts in my mind, in that heavy throaty voice.

"We'd like to ask you about George Thomson. His girlfriend has reported him missing, and she mentioned that he might be coming here, to visit you?"

Keane approves of me taking a long, long sip of my tea. With that stupid grin on his face like we're best pals.

"Have you heard from him?" Davis presses.

I shake my head. "I moved here to get away from them. I'm

not sure how much the other officers told you, but they're not good people."

"People?" Davis says sharply. She's keen, this one. Maybe she's trying to get a pay rise – no, a promotion. She sees herself as a detective.

"A figure of speech." This comes from Mr Smiles. He's doing my job for me, and Davis doesn't look too pleased.

"I was referring to the people I left behind," I tell Davis, wondering what she'd say if I revealed I'd never met them: only the two I killed.

It's like Sadie said at the beginning, this is just too mental to enter anybody's mind.

"You were an associate of George Thomson," Davis says.

"I was one of his drug-addicted punching bags, if that's what you mean."

Keane flinches humanely, and I see my chance – then seize it. "You can arrest me for that if you want. But it's true. He got me addicted to drugs, a little weed at first, and then the big stuff, the powder, the pills, the needles. And then, when I was good and out of it…"

Keane's face crinkles as I go on, letting a crackle into my voice, the beginning of a sob.

"He'd do whatever he wanted. And he'd let his friends go ahead and take their turns, too."

"Miss Newington," Davis says.

She doesn't look as moved, but there's some panic in her eyes. Maybe she's thinking about possible complaints.

"I came here to *escape* them, that life. I've been sober for almost a month. That's the longest in a long, long time. My sponsor says stress is bad for me."

"You're in AA?" Davis asks, her voice softening now. "My brother is in recovery. Where do you go?"

Nope. I'm not giving them something they can disprove. "I keep my addiction private, thank you."

The corner of her lip: a twitch. She knows something's up. I think she would make an excellent detective.

"Have you seen him, Sadie?" Keane says.

"No, and I hope I never do again."

"Are you surprised that he'd tell his girlfriend he was visiting you?" Davis asks, and then that lip twitching. She might as well say, *Because you didn't* seem *surprised.*

"I wish I could say I was, but he warned me he'd try to find me. How did *you* find me?"

That was a silly question. Davis places her tea down softly, keeps her head bowed, but raises her eyes. "Is there a reason you'd prefer for the police to not be able to find you?"

The man looks at her as if she's just lit herself on fire. She catches herself, *no no*, bad wannabe detective. I can almost hear her thoughts, and I realise that's a bad thing to let myself think. It's like reality splitting through my ears, threatening to tear. Like it did right here, but now my knuckles would pommel the top of a police officer's hat until it became a misshapen bowl.

"That is absolutely disgusting," I say, utterly dignified. "To throw my drug addiction in my face."

"I didn't—"

"Just because I've suffered, it doesn't mean I'm a criminal. Okay, yes, I've broken some drug laws. But I've been open about that. You look at me, you see a junkie whore. You probably think I'm a prostitute too, right? And that I stab grannies for spare change?"

They keep trying to speak, but each time, I push on. It's insane how genuinely angry I am; it's like Dad's voice is booming out of me.

"That's absolutely sick. Please, I'd like you to leave."

Keane stands straight away. Davis narrows her eyes at me for a significant moment, and I imagine her thinking about it later, pondering her career.

"I didn't mean to upset you," she says. "We'll be in touch if we need more information."

"Please, don't."

Arms folded, I hound them to the door, watching to make sure they've gone, then close it. I turn away – as the door crashes open.

Elizabeth strides into my flat. One of her favourite tricks. "What did they want?"

Pieces click together in my mind, as I stare at this woman: my partner in crime. But I'm not sure I want a partner, and this woman doesn't make me feel like a daughter at all.

## 66

## SADIE

*You won't have to be Charlotte for much longer.*

I stare down at the note, lovingly placed next to the coffee Malcolm has left for me. Maybe this is his way of making up for what he did at the torture hut, the place we're going to – if he has his way – do warped things.

The so-called poetry club is due to happen in two nights. Two evenings of whatever excitement and games Malcolm wants to indulge in, and then... Things that would make George seem tame.

I don't drink the coffee. Pills and powders weren't the only things I quit when I discovered I was pregnant. But I do *stare* at the pills in the box, the ones meant to knock out Malcolm's chosen girl... the ones which would look so juicy and horribly tempting lined up. Even thinking this is a stupid, dangerous thing to do. It's like I'm meditating on them, rehearsing the movements in my mind: crack the casing, cut the powder, snort, dream, bliss.

The landline rings, breaking apart my unhelpful thoughts. "Hello?"

"Lorna?" It's Rachael. I cringe at her voice; the last time I saw her, Malcolm was deciding whether or not to assault her. "Are you there?"

"Yes, it's so nice to hear from you."

"Is it? I wasn't sure if I should ring."

"Honestly, I'm so glad you did."

"Just after I embarrassed myself the other night…"

"Hmm," I say vaguely, could be an agreement or a question or anything she decides on.

"Malcolm told me what happened. You don't have to be polite."

"There's no use dragging it up."

"But I wanted to say sorry. I was just so drunk. And Malcolm was a complete gentleman. He rang you. Another woman to take care of me."

I'm guessing this means Malcolm told Rachael that she came onto him, sloppy drunk, and then I took her home. Fine, let her think it. God, Malcolm is just filth.

"And thank you," Rachael goes on. "After that, I didn't expect *this*. You and Malcolm are truly good people."

"Expect what?"

My heart has just started beating pretty damn fast. Pieces slotting together in my mind.

"Malcolm said you were the one who arranged it. The sale."

I smile, then remind myself to focus. Can't slip-up here. "Yes, I did."

"It's so, so nice of you. This is going to make such a difference to our lives."

Does Malcolm have it in him to feel love for the child he has with her? Somehow, I don't think so, despite what Lorna said about him being *very sensitive*. He seems pure demon to me.

"I hope you're being clever with the money."

"Uh… what do you mean?"

"Don't deposit it in a bank. Only spend in small amounts. Have you looked into getting a safety deposit box yet?"

"N-no," she says, sounding off-balance. "Do you think I should?"

"Well, yes, Rachael, I really do." I'm the most condescending bitch who's ever condescended. "Doesn't that seem like a smart idea to you? What if you were burgled? Or what if somebody broke in and held you hostage until you gave them the cash?"

"Do you really think that could happen?"

"It happens all the time. I can help you, if you like. Come with you to arrange everything."

"You really are a good person, Lorna."

"I try to be."

And it's the truth. I try. But I'm not going to have that luxury with Rachael.

## 67

# LORNA

"I just don't understand why they would be asking about me," Elizabeth says, her hand on her forehead like she's an actress in a melodrama. She's repeated herself several times already. "They didn't give *any* reason why?"

I take a sip of my coffee, shaking my head innocently. "It was all very confusing. They were asking how often you leave, what times you come home. Things like that."

"Hmm." Elizabeth drums her fingernails against the counter. Something about the way she looks at me tells me she's thinking about the dashcam footage. That's still a problem. "I'll need to get to the bottom of this."

"Could it be somebody from your past messing with you?" I ask. "Maybe they've reported you for something. Honestly, this is the last thing we need."

"It does affect both of us," she says pointedly. Bitch. "There are some possibilities. Sadie might be one. She's not exactly happy about the way we left things."

Yeah, and I'm sure that had nothing to do with Elizabeth forcing Sadie to watch her kill people.

"Maybe I'll talk to her. But that could make them suspicious…"

"Should we cancel our plans with Malcolm?" I ask.

*This* annoys her, which was sort of the point. "Don't tell me you're getting second thoughts."

"It's not that," I say – I lie; I'm not sure yet. "I don't want anything to happen to you. You've survived this long, doing what you do, because you've been careful."

"But he has to die," Elizabeth snaps. "There's no way around it. That little *worm*, that *nothing*, that broken oh-so precious little lamb – his shattered soul, his hateful heart…" She's suddenly sermonising in her tone. "He has to *go*."

"I'll bring him to you then," I tell her. "You wait at the spot. We'll do him there."

"Oh, we'll *do* him, Lorna. We'll do lots of things to him."

Like it's a challenge. Like I'd ever choose him. That's how she's talking.

"That's fine with me. As long as you're not scared."

Elizabeth stands up straight. The loose skin around her neck tightens as she lifts her chin. "I'm not scared of anything."

# TEN PER CENT

I'm supposed to be in charge.

I had power over you. But it's all slipping away. I'm so angry, all the time, and I know there's only one way to make it stop. Kill or die.

I refuse to die. Not permanently but, before I go, I must drag you down with me. To Hell. That's where we're going. We both know it. For what I did. For what you did.

For what the people who hurt me did... And the ones who hurt them.

It's only ten per cent, or thereabouts, by the way. When they say the abusers have often been abused. Only ten per cent or maybe even fewer go on to hurt others. Most are good people. Not like us. We have no excuse.

If there are devils, we're them. I'm not sure if I'm sorry. But I know what I have to do.

# 68

## SADIE

"Are you sure you're all right? We can reschedule?" I ask, standing on Rachael's doorstep.

She's wearing tights with two ladders up one leg, her eyes puffy with mascara. "No – it's fine. That was today?"

"We arranged it. I've got the text."

"Relax. There's no need to be so official."

Without another word, she turns and walks into the house. It's like a stoned dance, the way she moves. She leads me into the living room, not bothering to apologise for the shoes and coats scattered all over the floor. Not that she has to. It's her home.

My money – but her house, her walls. But it's just more evidence of how high she is. Or still drunk. Something. My belly tightens when I see the coffee table. The white powder really stands out on the glass, smeared across it. It's slightly moist; I think she's spilled a glass of water.

Moist coke between the teeth, while pregnant – fuck that, *fuck that*.

"I guess you're in no state to arrange the safety deposit box, then."

I'm judging her, judging myself, the woman I was in the early days, when it was just partying. Maintaining a flat, getting a blackout every night to stop thinking about what Elizabeth made me watch, the fear, the abuse; that's who I was really running from.

George and the others, yes, but also *her*. Maybe mostly her.

Rachael stays on her feet, seeming suddenly full of energy. "I've been thinking about the other night."

"Okay…"

"I have a theory about what happened. Can you tell me if I'm being mental?"

"Where's Riley?"

"Somewhere safe. Somewhere away from you." She runs a hand through her hair, then it gets tangled in the sweaty locks and she winces as she removes it. "And your pervert husband. That's what happened, isn't it – he drugged me, you both… in that hotel room. And then he paid me the *hush money* and hoped I'd never… never say anything."

She's breaking down, shuddering into the seat. "You know Riley is his, don't you?"

"You told me."

"I don't remember," she whispers, seeming on the edge of devastation.

Walking forward carefully, I force myself to place a comforting hand on her shoulder. *Force*, because she still reminds me of me. And there's a unique smell in the room; drugs, chemicals, booze, stale, disgusting, oblivion. A mantra – *my baby matters more. I'm supposed to be the good sister.*

She looks at my hand. "Get off."

I take the sofa seat. "I didn't do anything to you. But I can't speak for Malcolm."

"He's your husband, and you *can't* speak for him when he might have… and he has before…"

I swallow. "Me too."

"But you're still with him."

Not for much longer. Not when I get that money. "It's complicated."

"Complicated," Rachael repeats, shaking her head. "Like I'm a whore. My cousin was a sex worker for a while. And one Christmas, I called her that. A fucking *whore*, and everybody went mental at me. But that's the thing – it's the way I feel."

I'm not sure she believes this. Her neck and cheeks are turning red, like she's desperately trying not to cry, a coked-up rage. She springs to her feet, strides across the room, pulls open a drawer so roughly the whole cabinet shifts up and almost falls.

"I'm not his *fucking whore*," she screams, and then she does something very stupid.

She's holding a wad of cash, a few bills sticking out of the brown paper bag, more visible through a couple of small holes. And in her other hand – the stupid bitch, for Christ's sake… she's got a lighter, and she's moving it slowly toward the money. That's freedom. A chance for my baby.

"Rachael, don't do anything you'll regret."

"But that's it, isn't it?" She breaks my heart when her eyes fill with tears. "He gave me this money as a payment, for whatever he did with me, *to* me. I know that's what it is."

Closer and closer, the flame moving toward the bag. I'm maybe five feet away, a couple of big steps, then grab the bag, grab her other wrist. I'm doing junkie fight logic here, the fight-or-flight over the next hit.

"Please, just stop."

She pauses movement of the flame. "Did he put you up to this, then? Is he waiting outside? What's the plan, hit me then take the money?"

She resumes movement of the flame towards the bag, I rush forward. It's all planned out in my head. Grab her wrist – grab the bag…

And then she stumbles back and her head cracks on the doorframe, her skull splitting, a large chunk coming away, as I slowly comprehend that I've jumped across the room and pushed her hard in the chest.

Both hands – as hard as I can. I was aiming for her hands. But I've hit her chest and now she's lying on her side. She's rolled partially away from the door. Her hand twitches next to the lighter and a drop of blood and what could be – no, God no – bone.

Vomit spews up, and I'm sick on the lighter, fuck, sick on her hand a little bit. I turn away, puke all over the carpet, fall to my knees, gasping, useless.

I've got to call *999*. I go for my phone, and then she lets out this really shaky wheeze.

Crawling over to her – why can't I walk – I stare at her lifeless face. Her eyes staring at *nothing*, and it brings me back to the journalism, Elizabeth, and now I'm panting and I can't make it stop.

It's all distance – everything, reality. I see my hand stroke through her hair, over the matted blood and exposed insides, and I tell it to stop. But I can't feel it, let alone control it. I watch as my gaze becomes the table, and then the white powder, and my fingers smear all over the glass, picking up the powder.

I don't taste it as I rub my finger between my teeth. Hating myself, screaming, and then watching as I collect more, rub more, not a single goddamn worry about the effect it could have on my baby. Just the need to not be here, floating, and it works – somehow.

I wipe my mouth and I pick up my phone again, but I don't call the police.

## 69

---

## LORNA

I'm just returning from the shop – with wine; tonight's *the night* and I don't know what to do – when I get really pissed off. PC Davis is waiting for me at the entrance to our building, leaning against her car.

She's got this shit-eating grin on her face, like some police get. They're so convinced of their own power. So smug about it, and anytime they do a basic human nicety or kindness, they act like they're blessing you.

"This must be the most popular police hangout in Bristol," I say, as she waves and strolls over.

"I was wondering if you'd had a think about your friend, George Thomson? We've had reports he was seen in the local area recently."

"I don't know anything about that."

"It's just a coincidence he was so close by?"

I'm so not in the mood for this. Sometimes, as wrong as it is, I want to return to my old life. I thought it was a prison but – no, it is, *was*.

But at least then I had nothing but waking and sleeping and yoga and reading and...

"I guess it must be."

"No need for the tone," Davis says, that grin getting bigger.

"I didn't have a tone."

"Oh, I thought I heard one. I'm sorry."

"No, you didn't."

Davis tilts her head. "Excuse me?"

"You didn't think I had a tone. You're trying to antagonise me, probably because you heard it on some podcast somewhere." This is bad – I'm not even bothering with the accent, and now her eyes are narrowed like a wannabe detective. Back to English. "It's pathetic. You're harassing me just because you can."

"What was that?"

I sigh darkly. Her tone is becoming so condescending. Like she's so clever for catching me out.

"Your accent," she goes on.

"I don't know what you're talking about." I move to walk past her, but she steps subtly in my way. "Are you going to tackle me next, detective?"

She looks like she might hit me for a second, then snaps, "Keep that tone respectful and we won't have any problems."

In my mind, Dad, the abuser, the thief, the conman, and sometimes, the comedian, before I knew I had to hate him. Before I connected *it* with *him*. Oinking as he said, "Me a policeman, me so tough..." and my child's mind finding it the funniest thing ever somehow. I don't anymore.

"What problem? You can't arrest me for having a *tone* you don't like."

"We'll have to see about that."

"Oh, so we're going to *see* if you can arrest me."

"Hey – step back."

She raises her hands, though I'm nowhere near her, and then looks like she's about to go for her *radio*. She's acting like I'm some kind of a threat. It's insane.

"Put that down."

She takes her hand off the radio, gesturing at my carrier bag. Two bottles of wine. Sue me; I was going to get drunk.

"My shopping?"

"Just calm down."

I'm not doing anything to not seem calm. She's all wide-eyed and frantic, just because I made that detective comment. Snagged on a sore point.

"I'm going inside."

"Wait a second."

"I'm nowhere near you."

I walk even closer to the wall. We're in a narrow passageway with the flats on one side and tall hedges behind the wall on another. She rushes after me, jogs ahead and then spins, raising her hand.

"I said *wait*."

"What are you doing? I'm literally just walking into my flat."

"You've behaved in a threatening manner and you've ignored my direct instructions."

"Are you broken in the head, you fucking pig?"

This is bad. I'm shouting now, which is just what she wants, what this whole thing has been about.

"You need to calm down."

"Get fucked. You're a loser." I have to stop, but I can't. "Trying to get a promotion so you can pretend you don't hate yourself."

"Right, that's it…"

She strides forward and, I swear to God, her hand is going to her *belt*, to the cuffs or the baton or who knows what else. I turn and run down the passageway; there's another cut-through that leads to the park. I'm running fast, just on instinct, and I know it's a mistake. I know it makes me look guilty.

But that's what we did, when they came. We ran, me and Dad. Davis is faster. She catches up to me, one hand grabbing my arm.

I turn at the momentum, and I don't mean to do it. I don't *try*, but my instincts kick in and I swing the plastic bag, heavy with the two wine bottles. She gasps before they *clunk* against the bottom of her chin, don't break. They knock her head backwards. Her eyes saucer in shock, and she seems conscious as she's falling, almost annoyed at herself.

Then her head slaps off the hard concrete. Hard. Probably enough to give her a concussion at least.

I scan the area. Nothing, nobody, not yet. Are there cameras on the main street? Do police wear cameras on them in England? I don't think so; I *should* know. "PC Davis?" I murmur.

"Uh, uh," she whimpers. "Uh."

*Fuck.* I tap down her pockets, take out her phone. She keeps moaning as I call *999*. This is bad; I can't leave her here without calling an ambulance.

*Never* bring the police down on you by hurting one of their own. But if she survives... *Fuck.*

I put the phone down, drop it, run down the street. Keep running until I'm about to be on the main road, then slow to a walk and turn into the park. Cut across it, taking out my mobile as I steadily make my way toward the city. I need help.

# 70

## SADIE

"How did you get here so fast?" I ask, cringing when Elizabeth walks through the back door. She hurries inside and slams it behind her, waving a hand at me, and I move away. She's freaking me out. Everything is, especially the corpse in the living room. And the fact I'm high, floating, hurting my baby with every breath, and I can't make it stop. "We have to go to a hospital."

Elizabeth grins, seeming energised, like this is the day she's been waiting for. And it is: for me to become like her. She doesn't even have to say it. We both know. "I thought she was already dead."

"I think she is. But for me."

Elizabeth claps me on the arm. When I cringe and leap away, she laughs meanly. "Oh, Sadie, you silly little slattern. Are you high again?"

"Please."

"Poisoning your precious baby with all that filth?"

"P-Please." I spread my hands over my belly. "Don't say that. It's not – I'm not."

"We can't go to a hospital until we've dealt with this. Let's see then."

Hands on her hips in the living room, she stares down at the body. The broken thing with the split skull. The cash isn't there, though. It's in my pocket. I wonder how I should feel about myself, that I thought to do that. "An accident?"

"Obviously."

Elizabeth tuts and shakes her head. "So dirty. This is going to be quite the clean-up. But we have to wait until it's dark. And I need you to do something for me."

I stare in disbelief at Rachael, the ladders in her tights, her legs resting at unnatural angles. "We can't just leave her here."

"We can. She won't start to smell for a few hours."

"But she has a child. She has people who might have keys. Might find her."

Elizabeth groans. "I suppose you're right. Ah, God. We'll have to store her body on the floor in the kitchen. But first we need a towel or a rag or something we can burn later. To catch any more blood. Then we'll clean in here, wrap her up... for *fuck's* sake, Sadie."

She darts forward, raising her hand. I yell and flinch away.

"Shut *up*," Elizabeth says. "If I'm late, I'm going to hurt you. And when I do this, you *owe* me, you stupid, stupid, pathetic, snivelling girl. Go get a towel."

"Late for what?" I ask.

My cheek stings when she slaps me, and I think, very slowly, how hypocritical it is to tell me to be quiet and then make a loud *slap* noise like that. "Towel, now."

Halfway up the stairs, I start choking on my sobs, my belly cramping. My baby. I'm high and there's a life inside of me. My son or daughter. My child. Step by step, I keep going.

# 71

## LORNA

"What are we going to do?"

"We'll sort it, but first we have to take care of something."

"No – we have to go now. We have to start again."

"I'm telling you what's happening. You're lucky I've even forgiven you."

"You're lucky I'm here."

"Either way, we've got to do this first. I've waited long enough. I'm done. It has to end."

"Waited for what? What are you talking about?"

"You really haven't guessed yet? Christ."

"What?"

"You're stupider than I thought."

"I'm leaving if you carry on."

"Listen, I'm sorry. I'll keep you safe. It's my job."

"Th-Thank you."

"I love you."

"I love you too."

I've got a knife hidden in my pocket.

# 72

## SADIE

We're out in the middle of nowhere, the sun just starting to set, Elizabeth pacing up and down next to a suspicious patch of dirt.

I keep thinking I should ask about that, but I can't think about anything except I wish I could kill this bitch. And myself.

If I've killed my baby with this filth…

"They'll be here soon," Elizabeth says. "Go hide in the bushes over there, next to the gate. When they get here, I'll tell them the gate's broken and they'll have to climb it. When they turn, hit him over the head, hard, Sadie. I know you can do this. I always knew you had it in you."

Rachael's body is still in the boot of Elizabeth's car, parked just a few feet away.

"But they'll see your car in here," I say, thinking of dashcams, possible witnesses to the arrival of our vehicles, all of that, the big powerful fist of the law smashing me across the face. "They'll know the gate isn't broken."

"I can say I broke it when I closed it. The clasp stuck. Don't overthink it. Take this."

She hands me a garden trowel, smiling like I'm the best daughter she ever could've asked for.

———

I can't call this paranoia. I've got every reason to fixate on this weird pulsing in my body. Everything rushing around, numb and tingling then suddenly so full of nerves it's almost too much. I grip the trowel's handle hard, enough for my knuckles to turn white.

A car is pulling up the narrow path. Malcolm sits at the front and, at his side, small and somehow sad-looking, is Lorna.

"What's the hold-up?" Malcolm says.

"The gate's broken. We'll have to walk around."

"What the hell is this?" Lorna says, looking between them, then settling on Malcolm. "You shouldn't know about this place."

"Oh, Lorna, my sweet angel. I really love you. Honestly."

*"Explain."*

"It's simple. This is the spot Elizabeth told *you* would be my grave. But really, she wants us – me and her, that is, darling – to kill *you*. Isn't that so, Lizzie?"

Elizabeth waves a hand. "It's all lies. Why would I want to kill my beloved daughter?"

"Because you're a deranged hag."

"How do you two know each other?"

"Oh, Elizabeth has done lots of damage to me, Lorna. More than you could imagine. But I've come to appreciate her over the years. She's helped me in certain ways."

Even through my high haze, I listen closely. I'm slowly creeping through the shadows toward the path. Lorna and Malcolm have their backs to me, Elizabeth side-on.

"I don't understand."

"She's a freak, and I happened to grow up around her. She was quite a pretty lady then, if you can believe it. She took an interest in little Malcolm, all right, but it's okay. She helped me after. With money, connections, you."

"M-me?" Lorna says.

I am so goddamn angry. Elizabeth has been doing this for years, manipulating me and now my sister, clearly. That seems to matter, the fact she's my sister, as I rush from the shadows with the trowel held over my head. Maybe it's because I can feel my baby pumping so vitally in me, or a rage driven by the drugs, the truth.

We're just her playthings.

"Sadie, don't you d—"

It's almost funny, that she would use that phrase – or try to. *Don't you dare.* She's been daring me since the day we met.

The flat side of the trowel bounces off the top of her head, once, twice – she raises her hand. I hit her again, and then she slumps backward with her arms falling limp.

# 73

## MALCOLM

I haven't laughed like this in years.

She comes sprinting from nowhere and hits the old hag over the head. It's still odd, seeing Sadie in the flesh. Lizzie showed me photos before, but seeing her for the first time was different. I'm used to it now, though, and can tell the difference between her and Lorna. There are subtle tics, even in the way Sadie shudders when she steps away from Lizzie's body.

"Fucking... bitch," Sadie whispers, her voice shaking, so much more fragile than Lorna could ever be. "I'm done doing what you want me to do!"

That all comes out as a melodramatic yell, her hands shaking like an infant's. That was just one of the many giveaways, her weakness, her inability to fight back. It was unattractive and a clear sign she wasn't Lorna.

"Thanks, Sadie." I grin. "I was going to do that, but you saved me the effort."

"How did she give me to you? That's what you said."

I meet Lorna's eyes with a crooked smile. "Darling, there's an elderly lady bleeding to death. Please have some humanity."

She steps forward, all Scottish sass, all fire, all heat. I used to love her – I still do, even if I was debating leaving her in the same ditch as her birth mother. She might as well know; she might die soon.

"Lizzie did some bad things, groomed me, is the modern term. Made me her little disciple. She had videos of me... well, doing stuff she made me do. And then one day, she told me she had twin daughters, that she'd been watching them for years. Your dad was abusive, she said, so I was told to help you with that. And so I did, and we got married, and opened the box – and she heard about some of it. Asked, I told her. She was proud."

"Proud?" Sadie whispers, as if this moment is in any way hers. "How could she be proud of that?"

"Proud of me, mostly." There's something so funny about their little shocked faces, so similar. "She's always wanted proof there was something special about her, in her blood. A true predator. But you two were disappointments. I'm the one who manipulated you, Lorna. And Sadie – your act was a joke."

She flinches. "You knew?"

"The whole time. Lorna would never let me use her body as roughly as you did. And your blow jobs are way too bloody enthusiastic."

She blushes, something else Lorna rarely does. "You're not human."

"You manipulated me." Lorna steps up to me. "She told you to seduce me, and so you did... because you're her little pet?"

"I don't think *pet* is very flattering. But yes. She wanted me to take care of your daddy. But, more importantly, wanted *you* to take care of him with me. She liked it when I told her how dark I could make you go – watching me do certain things to certain young ladies. How you'd goad me. Get me going."

"That's because *I* was the one in charge," Lorna snaps, and she could be telling the truth; she could mean it. I can't tell. "I used you. I'm the one who wanted to..."

"Kill. Those. Bitches. You can't even say it. No. Don't be so hard on yourself. I mean it. I did that. I manipulated you into helping me. You're a poor little victim."

She's not a fan of that word. "I'm not a victim. I'm the one who suggested the box. I wanted those girls dead."

"No – you didn't. You were never in control."

"I forced *you* to do it."

"You're a scarred, scared little girl, a product of too much attention from Daddy. The truth is, you're a cliché. I walk past you and drop a paper cup of coffee, when you're supposed to be hiding and watching me… and you still can't help but pick it up. Or smile when I turn and catch you. Do you think I really wouldn't know you? A mask, glasses, an accent, a haircut… none of it can change the fact I *own* you, Lorna."

I beam down at her, and there's nothing she can do about it.

She knows it's true, remembers me approaching her. She even let me hug her, and then we talked, and I explained. She was mine and always would be; I knew about the twin.

She might want me to cry about what Elizabeth did, but there's no use in that. I rarely even think about it. And as long as Lorna has kept me supplied with young fun, I haven't cared to address the problem.

But now she's in my life again – I should thank Sadie… Ooh… maybe I should take Sadie and Lorna at the same time.

I can imagine Sadie bent over, properly bouncing with Lorna's legs split open—

*Slice.*

Lorna opens my throat with something cold and metal.

I swear I hear that, the *slice* sound in the air, like it's a bloody samurai sword or something. And then I'm choking, something lodged in my throat, a giant congealed ball of blood inflating, and then she does it again, again, keeps cutting me, reality bleeding, darkness falling.

I'm going. There's so much I still want to do. But I'm not here anymore.

# THOSE DAYS

Malcolm, everything is dark.

It hurts. Please help me. I know I should've been kinder to you. I know I shouldn't have listened to those ugly voices whispering at me to do ugly things, to compel your body in novel and mentally disfiguring configurations.

I've hurt you. Made you please me. Hurt you. My head – and the dark... Please, let me back up. I can do better. I promise, I won't try to kill you. Malcolm, you would've been so different. Or the same. I'm not sure what made me. If I'm your God. If there is no God.

I can't climb out of this hole. There are no walls to press onto. There's no... oh, yes, *yes*, there is. There is! I can see it. Ha, ha, you fuck, you stupid little empty-headed *cunt*. Ha, ha, ha. I can see you in Hell, beneath me.

You're locked in a cage and there are devils all around you, red versions of me at various ages, whipping you and spitting acid at you and making your skin sizzle and your naked body scream and your mouth split open and your jaw dislocate and your lower lip stretch down and splinter and envelop yourself and now, I see it, the light, I'm awake, head fuzzy.

I can salvage this. I hate you. I'm going to fix this, somehow. Oh, those days... I remember how you blinked your puppy eyes up at me. I remember how you moaned just so, and the things you let me do with your...

Oh, those days.

# 74

## LORNA

I've killed my husband. I can reflect on it almost coldly as I sit next to the corpse, my hands covered in blood, my heart pounding and my heart hurting and...

I'm an idiot for going back to him, for ever thinking I'd let him get his claws into me again. He had me *defending* my part in what we did to those women, and I don't even know how. It's just him, his unique effect, but he's gone now. And Davis is probably dead. So that's a dead police officer too...

"P-proud of you," Elizabeth wheezes. I turn, staring at her in the setting orange sunlight. She manages to sit up, dizzy but alive, her eyes crossing as she gets her balance. She even smiles. "Really, I am. I always knew you had it in you."

"What did you do to him?" I say, my voice seeming very far away.

Sadie wraps her arms around her middle, staring shell-shocked at Elizabeth as though she's a corpse risen from the grave.

Elizabeth shrugs. "I was a young woman and he was an interesting little boy. I'm sure you can use your imagination."

"So you're just as bad as my dad, then. As Finn. As so many

sick *fucks* in this world who get off on abusing people too young to defend themselves. You're to blame, for h-him…"

My voice shudders, and suddenly I'm nearly crying. There's something almost alive about the way Malcolm watches me, except for the lack of blinking and the state of his neck.

"She's unforgivable," Sadie whispers.

"She was always right there." I laugh bitterly, shaking my head as I stare at our so-called mother. "Through Malcolm."

Elizabeth groans. "I think that's an extremely simplistic way to look at things. There are plenty of people who have experienced the sorts of things Malcolm did and grown up to be perfectly normal, healthy people. But Malcolm had certain desires in his blood – and I called to that. He wanted it. He never fought it."

"He laughed when I hit you over the head," Sadie says.

"He did?"

"Of course," I say. "Just like I laughed when Dad died."

"That's not the same." Elizabeth winces as she tries to stand, then sits back down. "Will one of you help me up, please?"

I stand, rising from my place next to Malcolm, and clean the knife on my trousers. I feel quite emotional as I reach out and touch Sadie's arm. She flinches – maybe because my hands are bloody – but doesn't move away.

"Sadie, we went about this all wrong. I can see it now. We've both been victims of this woman and her bullshit. She's been torturing me for years – through Malcolm. And you, through the *journalism…*"

Sadie shakes, nodding, a single tear gliding down her cheek. "Lorna, I took drugs. Powder. I don't know what it was. My baby…"

There's a plan forming in my mind, but it means relying on people I'd happily kill if the circumstances were different. "Don't beat yourself up," I tell her, rubbing her shoulder, spreading blood all over her top. "It's *them*."

"And – I killed a woman... she's in the boot. Oh, God. It's Rachael."

I sigh, processing it quickly. Poor Rachael, and poor Riley – I never wanted that for Malcolm's child. An orphan.

"It was an accident," Sadie whispers. "But I did it."

"We'll have to deal with that." At least the body is here.

"D-Deal with it?" Elizabeth says, struggling to stand again, groaning when she drops onto her ass. "Help me."

"I say we kill this bitch," I snap, staring at my double, at my eyes which look so naïve in Sadie's face, my mouth which is somehow trusting with her lips.

"I don't think I can," Sadie says. "I'm done with it all."

"That's all right. I can do it. And then – me, you, together. We'll fight for your baby... as sisters, okay?"

"Do I have to be here? When you..."

I shake my head, wiping the knife on my trousers again. Elizabeth raises her hands, then tries to scoot backwards on her bum.

"I always knew there was something wrong with Malcolm. He wouldn't talk about his childhood much, but there was always a hint of darkness there."

"Your father was a tramp," Elizabeth spits, looking demented and... weak, honestly. "A dirty nobody. A junkie."

"Those are some fine last words, Mother."

"Wait, just you wait a—"

Reality isn't bleeding this time. I'm fully conscious as I roughly drag the Stanley blade across her neck, opening her up, and then lacerate her until the struggling stops. When it's over, I stand, looking down at the mess I've made. More murder in the past couple of weeks than in my entire life before that. I'm sick of the stench of blood.

"Thank you," Sadie says softly. "She deserved it. But I don't think I could have..." Sadie places her hands on her hips, letting out a trembling breath. The last of the sunlight is just leaving us, the world kissed crimson.

"We have to disappear," I tell her. "Between Rachael, Jonesy, George—"

"Jonesy and George are *dead*?"

"Yeah. Now Malcolm and Elizabeth. Christ, I'm a serial killer." Even to myself, my laughter sounds deranged. But I can't help it.

"What are we going to do?" Sadie whispers. "My baby…"

"There's a way. But we won't be able to go to a hospital."

"But—"

I touch her arm. "Would you rather be in prison? You'll be fine – you'll ride it out. Your baby will be fine. In the meantime, we have to disappear. And I know a way. After my niece or nephew is born, we'll work on the next steps."

"How can we *disappear*?" she says, as if she's tired of the whole thing.

"Did Rory ever mention a certain *favour*?"

I take out my phone, remove the SIM, snap it, then replace the battery. Then I take a photo of Malcolm's corpse.

"What are you doing?" Sadie says, sounding so spaced out, hardly even here.

"Rory has wanted Malcolm gone for years. What he did at Faraday – and before, when they were kids. He was worse than a bully. Rory made me an offer once. If I ever had enough, snapped, killed Malcolm, he'd make sure the police wouldn't find me. But he'll want proof."

"How can he make sure we're safe?"

"He has a bunker, he told me."

Sadie cringes. "He mentioned it once. It didn't sound nice."

"Better than prison. Or trying to travel the country with our faces plastered all over the place. Somebody probably saw me with the officer, or you and Elizabeth with Rachael… when Malcolm goes missing, I'll be questioned. Do you see how this works?"

She moves away from me, almost like she thinks I'm going to leap on her. "I get it. Okay."

"Hey, I don't mean to bully you. I'm not like her."

I gesture to our birth mum. Sadie turns to her – then looks away, covering her eyes.

"I can't look. What do we do now?"

"Bury the bodies. Drive to Scotland. We'll change cars a few times on the way, stick to back roads. It's risky, but we can do it."

"Why are you helping me?"

"I meant what I said. I've never had family before. Maybe we can be that. Maybe something good can come out of this."

"I think it could. Th-thank you, Lorna."

"Just – no more lies, all right?"

Sadie nods shakily. "No more lies."

# EPILOGUE

## Sadie
## One And A Half Years Later

I cradle Oliver to my chest, rocking him gently as the light breeze caresses us. I'll never tire of how beautiful the landscape is, the emptiness of it, the closest neighbours two miles away.

And Rory has cameras all around his perimeter. If the police ever come, we can hide, back underground, back to the bunker. I savour every one of Oliver's heartbeats as he sleeps against my chest. The wind calms him, the hush of the breeze through the grass, the groan of the skies.

At times like these, I can forget that Lorna is wanted for the assault of a police officer. And in connection with several missing persons cases. If the corpses are ever found…

We have a deal. If one of us is found, we'll confess to all of it, and the other one will raise and love Oliver. I kiss Oliver on the top of the head, savouring his baby smell, fresh guilt cutting into me when I think about what I did. The drugs, risking Oliver's little life.

He was born in a screaming war in the bunker, with Skye working as a surprisingly good midwife. If it wasn't for the *games* they insist we play as payment, I could almost like it here.

Back on the property, I slip through the gate and walk across the grassy field toward the stone structure. Hades comes galloping over, the energetic whippet with the dark orange fur. He settles down when he's close, sniffing the air.

"Careful, he's sleeping," I say, lowering Oliver.

Hades sniffs him and then walks at my side. Rory is sitting on the porch, one leg folded over the other. "Sadie, it's not your turn tonight, is it?"

"It's Lorna this week."

"Excellent. You were a little lacklustre last time. You should ask her for some tips."

I bite down, taking the insult, as we've had to take countless times. It's a choice between enduring what they make us do – the games are degrading, but sadly, Lorna and I can tolerate just degrading – or hope we can keep Oliver safe in the outside world.

As I walk by Rory, he casually grabs my leg. I spin, stare. "We said nothing outside the games, remember?"

He removes his hand, grinning. "Relax. I'm just messing around."

"I've got my son in my arms."

"You better get inside. Don't want to risk being out for too long."

I carry Oliver downstairs, into the cellar, and then open the bookcase door and walk down the narrow hallway. There are some BDSM sculptures on the walls, penises and breasts. There were more, but we removed what we could.

We're living in a perverted couple's converted sex dungeon. Better than prison, I guess. Lorna is reading a book in bed, her legs tucked beneath her. She's let her hair grow long, a braid draped over her shoulder. We've talked a lot since we came here, bonded even more, sharing stories of our childhoods and the pain we endured, our regrets, our mistakes.

We're both bad people. We've agreed on that. But we're trying to be better, in our own way. Seeing her with Oliver, I know we have something special. He reacts to her as he does to me, like we're the same person.

Lorna closes her book. "Shut the door, please."

I lay Oliver down. "Is something wrong?"

"I've had enough," she says, once I've closed the door. "I've been thinking about it. I think there's a way."

"To do what?"

"What else?" She leans forward. "Kill Rory."

THE END

## ALSO BY NJ MOSS

All Your Fault

———

Her Final Victim

———

My Dead Husband

———

The Husband Trap

———

The Second Wife

———

Through Her Eyes

———

Ruin Her Life

# A NOTE FROM THE PUBLISHER

**Thank you for reading this book.** If you enjoyed it please do consider leaving a review on Amazon to help others find it too.

**We hate typos.** All of our books have been rigorously edited and proofread, but sometimes mistakes do slip through. If you have spotted a typo, please do let us know and we can get it amended within hours.

**info@bloodhoundbooks.com**